E. G. Perry

A Trip Around Cape Cod

The South Shore and Historical Plymouth

E. G. Perry

A Trip Around Cape Cod
The South Shore and Historical Plymouth

ISBN/EAN: 9783337144999

Printed in Europe, USA, Canada, Australia, Japan

Cover: Foto ©Andreas Hilbeck / pixelio.de

More available books at **www.hansebooks.com**

A
Trip Around Cape Cod

The South Shore and
Historical Plymouth

Written by E. G. PERRY

A Cape Cod Boy

PRICE, $2.00

Copies can be obtained of E. G. PERRY, 69 State St., Boston; or at Residence, Monument Beach, Mass.

COPYRIGHTED MAY 21st, 1898

INTRODUCTORY.

THERE has been much said about Cape Cod, — its sandy soil and its queer people. Now, as a native-born Cape Codder, I am proud to think I can own this as my birthplace. I have done business in Boston with its business men, and with the business men of Cape Cod also, and think I have had an unusual opportunity to speak of the merits of each. I used to have a wholesale confectionery business in Boston and suburban towns, and I had for my customers some of the finest retail stores — elegant drug stores, with their plate-glass fronts, their magnificent soda fountains, and some of the best grocery and variety stores — and one would naturally say, "What splendid customers you have." But, alas! There is so much style in the fixtures and the living of some of the city people that, as a rule, some poor fellow supplying them with goods has got to be a good long waiter.

Now, I have traveled for Boston firms on Cape Cod. I had good trade, and never lost fifty dollars while on the route ; and I have done business on the Cape for myself, and can say for a truth there is no class of people, — north, south, east or west, — who are more willing or ready to meet their bills than the Cape Cod people.

Take a trip around the Cape with me, and mingle with the inhabitants. You will have a splendid vacation, and meet a people who for their sterling worth and honesty are not excelled by any people in the world.

Yours truly,

E. G. PERRY.

Residence of Jos. Jefferson.

A TRIP AROUND CAPE COD.

STARTING at Buzzards Bay station, we will find nestled there among its tall pines at Buttermilk Bay the stately residence of Joseph Jefferson, and as we have one-half hour to spare, let us take a drive around the grounds of our friend, the oldest actor in New England. We cannot help but think what a magnificent place, and if we meet Mr. Jefferson, we will find him such a fine, kind-hearted man, ever ready to do a kind act. He has surrounded himself by his sons and daughters and his dear friends. It is really a paradise on earth — this beautiful estate.

FROM here we can admire the view down the beautiful Buzzards Bay; from the bridge, on our route, we can see the fine Dorr estate with its beautiful buildings and its fine view of the water. Who would not really enjoy such a fine location? And here also we see the beautiful summer home of Colonel Taylor of Boston. Look at his well-kept grounds, and see the two new mansion houses he is building for his sons.

On Buzzards Bay.

Look again and see the world-wide known "Gray Gables," named by the distinguished and beautiful Mrs. Cleveland. With its forty acres of fine land, with its beautiful nativeness, and with its well-arranged drives and walks, and its distinguished look — for should it not look distinguished in having the honor of the President of the United States as its owner? — with the President coming here for five successive years and making long stops, does it not speak well for dear old Buzzards Bay?

Here we may see distinguished people who are being entertained by the President. His full Cabinet have been here, and many other very worthy and noted people. Not only does the President entertain his noted friends, but he comes, he and his wife, as summer residents.

Gray Gables, Buzzards Bay.   Residence of President Grover Cleveland.

Now just take a look at Mrs. Cleveland as she goes into our little country church and sits in the seat with some of her maids during church service.   See her stoop and kiss a kind Christian woman, a cripple who lives in this village, and who has to be brought to church in a chair when she does come.   This is only a small glimpse of the lady who has filled the exalted place of the first lady in the land.   Do you wonder, reader, why we feel so proud to have the Clevelands in our town as summer residents, when they have been so celebrated, and by their coming have made this old Cape Cod talked about and advertised as never before?   May peace and entire rest be theirs long to enjoy !*

* See letter in back of book.

8

Parker House, Buzzards Bay.

Residence of W. A. Nye, Bournedale.

9

IN leaving Buzzards Bay we drive along through a beautiful wooded country road. The trees are very tall each side of the way. Our next stop will be at Bournedale. The country view is exceedingly picturesque, there being a very high range of hills on either side. Bournedale is a beautiful little place nestled in among the hills, and a trim country village.

From here we drive to the next village, and we cannot but admire Sagamore. It is a place where the homes are all owned by their occupants, lawns well kept, houses well painted, and a most attractive

Residence of Hon. Isaac N. Keith, Sagamore.

country village. It is a part of the town of Bourne. Riding through Bourne we find its drives are remarkably fine, the town expending a large sum of money each year on its highways. We desire to be gracious to our summer friends, and give them the best of roads to ride on, for we realize they pay over sixty per cent of the taxes in our towns, and the only benefit they get is a few months' pleasure in the summer.

We leave Sagamore, and have then only about two and one-half miles to make before we arrive in the town of Sandwich ; that name sounds dear to us, for it was the original name of the town of Bourne.

We feel delighted when our former town prospers in any of its achievements. There is not on the whole Cape Cod a handsomer place than this old town. We find here some of the best farms there are anywhere in New England. It is here that the glassworks stand ; but we are very sorry to relate that they now stand idle. They have made here some of the finest glassware in the world, the pay-roll to its employees was for years very large, enabling the residents to own fine places. On the main street we see its fine old elms making an arch over the street,

Street View, looking towards Depot, Sandwich.

and think it is just simply grand. Then there are some beautiful lakes in the town, where for miles one can row or sail, and just drink in the beauties of nature. How wonderful it is that God has made such a beautiful earth for us to live on, and gives us our different seasons, that we may the more enjoy each season as it comes anew to us ; my heart goes out to Him in reverence and praise as I look upon the many beautiful and wonderful works of nature.

11

Congregational Church, Sandwich.

The Weston and Belcher Places, Sandwich.

Lower Shawme Lake, Sandwich.

High School, Sandwich.

LEAVING Sandwich and taking a short drive, we find ourselves in a village called Quaker Village. Here one feels really purer and better in looking upon the homes of these kind-hearted Quaker people. How good some of the ladies look, and how peaceful the little old men in their broad-brimmed hats! They have always looked to me from childhood as a very impressive, gentle and kind-hearted people. Although I never went to one of their services, still I have always felt like paying reverence to their religion.

Farm of George Hoxie, East Sandwich.

WE next drive to West Barnstable, and all along the route we find exceptionally fine farms; the people who own them have their quaint way of living, but are enjoying this life really more than they are aware of. This is a very handsome place, has streets well laid out, and houses well cared for; one would imagine he was in some fine manufacturing village, everything looks so new and bright. From here we can take the stage for Marston's Mills, Cotuit, and Centreville, places which we will visit later.

Church at West Barnstable.

As we leave this quiet village, we can look away down over the marsh and see the farmer with his men getting in his winter's supply of hay, making it in great stacks; for the crops are always so large that, although having big barns, they cannot contain all that they gather. As we drive along, we see some fine cranberry bogs which bring many hundreds of dollars to the people about these villages.

In the fall they have the huskings — how the young people enjoy helping to husk the corn! — and you see the shy boy who has found a red ear edging along to his favored maid to give her a sly kiss for the red ear, and then a general laugh goes up from the merry ones and they

scamper about for a good time, till the old farmer will call out, "Boys,
boys!" — then all is still again until another red ear is found. They
often have a molasses-candy pull. What fun these boys and girls have!
How they enjoy life and never realize it!

Finally we arrive in the town of Barnstable, our County seat on the
Cape, and we find here a good place to rest our horses, while we partake of a
good dinner at Mr. Phinney's, the genial storekeeper, who also keeps the
hotel. Often we have stayed here over night and had a quiet night's
sleep, after spending a delightful evening with Mr. and Mrs. Phinney. It
is here we have our Court House and County Jail, but we are proud to
say there are not many disturbances on our Cape, and we do not usually
have a very full house at our jail.

Barnstable Court House.

Passing through Barnstable we drive along for a few miles on a fine
street shaded by trees and with a beautiful sea view. This is a very
attractive country.

View at Barnstable.

SOON we arrive in the village of Yarmouthport, and here indeed we find remarkable streets and very attractive houses. In this place our representative to Congress, Mr. John Simpkins, has his beautiful country estate. As we drive along through this fine village, we cannot help but to exclaim what a beautiful coast Cape Cod has, especially through Yarmouthport.

Continuing on our journey, we drive through quite a piece of woods through which is now laid out a beautiful macadamized road for about six miles, and find ourselves at North Dennis. We would not pass this place by without a word, for this is the village where the Nobscusset House is situated, one of the largest and best hotels on Cape Cod, patronized principally by wealthy Western people, its location and equipments are the best. In the village of North Dennis the houses are well kept and well cared for.

17

Nobscussett House, Dennis.

Now we take our last ride for the day, for when we arrive at the village of East Dennis, we must call at the house of Mr. Samuel Chapman. We are by this time weary and tired, and go in to find, always, a welcome here. Many are the traveling men, weary from the day's toil and ride, who have stopped at this very hospitable place. The house is a very large, well-kept one, both inside and out, with many acres of land well cultivated by Mr. Chapman and his help. He keeps about ten fine cows, so you can have plenty of good, pure milk to drink. The table is set with everything from their own farm, Mrs. Chapman is a fine cook, and there is a general air of refinement about the house. We go to our clean, comfortable room for the night, and, after a delightful rest, awake in the morning at the call for breakfast, and again partake of some of those delicious biscuits made by the lady herself.

Our team is brought to the door, we jump in and say good-by, and start this time for Orleans, but before we have gone far we come to Brewster. Here we find some elegant summer homes of rich and retired people. The main street is very beautiful, one of the finest on the Cape. The cottages owned by the native people are kept in an unusual state of cleanliness and neatness. Driving along through this town we come to the very finest place on the Cape, owned by Mr. Nickerson of Chicago, who is a native of Cape Cod. The barn on this estate is better than most houses. This place, by the way, was built by one of our most honored townsmen, Mr. M. C. Waterhouse, of Bourne.

Town Hall, Brewster.

Baker's Pond, Brewster.

Residence of Hon. Roland Nickerson, East Brewster.

Stable of Hon. Roland Nickerson, East Brewster.

Summer Residence of Mr. Crosby, East Brewster.

Shattuck House, Orleans.

Soon after passing other fine estates, we go through a few miles of woods and find ourselves in the town of Orleans. This active little village has the appearance of a much larger town. Everything here is thrifty and always busy. We drive at once to the Shattuck House and receive a warm welcome. That is why this hotel is so much patronized by the traveling men. At the stable one can always find any kind of a team with a good, careful driver. We are always pleased to come again to Orleans, for it is here we have made many acquaintances, and many are the pleasant evenings spent at the Odd Fellows Hall. If you ever wander down this way, reader, you will find this a delightful little village located in the center of Cape Cod, ninety-four miles from Boston. The scenery in the town is beautiful, the houses are well painted and the fine lawns well kept — everything in the town denotes thrift. It is bounded on the east by the Atlantic Ocean, and a river for a distance of four miles extends into the village. Here all kinds of fish can be found

View at Orleans.

Residence of J. H. Sparrow, Orleans.

Old Mill at Orleans.

The Snow Library, Orleans.

in good numbers; also there is good bathing and boating. The principal industry is manufacturing of clothes. The French-Atlantic Cable Co. have a plant here, and the schools are especially fine. They have a town hall and library, and are also well represented in having several good churches. Summer houses are always in good demand in this busy little village.

Snow's Block, Orleans.

Here we leave our horses for a rest, and take the train for the tip end of Cape Cod, Provincetown. By train, we have quite a ride through several little villages, passing through the handsome village of Wellfleet, which, by the way, is getting to be quite a summer place. Then we pass through the Truros, very much noted, as along its shores they have had so many wrecks, considered by mariners the most dangerous place on the Massachusetts coast.

Billingsgate Light, Wellfleet.

View at Wellfleet.

Wellfleet Light.

Congregational Church, Wellfleet.

28

View of Wellfleet.

Hotel at Wellfleet. Holbrook House.

Wreck of Four-Masted Schooner, Daniel B. Fearing, Wellfleet.

Naucett Life Saving Station, near Eastham.

In going down on the train, it seems as if there was no end to the Truros, North Truro, East Truro, West Truro, and Truro, and if there was any point on the compass not named, I think it would be another Truro. Now we come in view of the old ocean. We can see the water on each side of us. At some points it is only a few miles across, and looking ahead we see several church spires, and soon behold

View at Provincetown.

this much talked of place, Provincetown, which stands out on a prominent point of land nearly surrounded by water. It is at this station the boys and girls, and even the men and women, come regularly to see the trains arrive. We look around for comfortable quarters to stop in while in this far-distant town from Boston, and if we decide to stop at the Atlantic House, we will be met at the door by the proprietor, Mr. Smith, and his big hand is always extended to his friends. A right glad welcome one always gets.

31

FRANK SMITH,
Proprietor Atlantic House, Provincetown.

We wash after our long journey and then go in to dinner. I can see the proprietor with his white apron, and his white cap on his head, saying, "Well, gentlemen, what will you have? Give us a big order, for we have on the bill of fare clam chowder, baked blue fish, roast lamb, green peas, sweet corn, mashed potato, strawberry shortcake, pudding, watermelon," etc. I do believe that of all Cape Cod places, the traveling men, and tourists also, will all declare there is no place like the Atlantic House, for the proprietor really enjoys standing and cracking a joke, and he also enjoys seeing his guests partake of a dinner as if it tasted good to them. After dinner many are the amusing stories Mr. Smith always has ready to tell. Here we do not mind if we have to stop over Sunday or for a few days in so delightful a place and with such genial people.

Highland Light and Cliff.

Town Hall and View at Provincetown.

33

Rounding Cape Cod.

Residence of Mr. Snow, Orleans.

Returning we take the train and get off again at Orleans. We here have our horses hitched up and drive through this pleasant village, taking a four miles' drive over a rather sandy road, in fact the poorest we have seen since leaving Buzzards Bay.

Namequoit River, South Orleans.

Our first stop is at South Orleans. Here we find Post-Office and store combined, and we are surprised to find so fine an assortment in this country store. Near by is Pleasant Bay. This is a wonderfully attractive location situated on a high bluff seventy-five feet above sea level, with beautiful sandy beach free from stones, with bathing facilities excellent. Here is a beautiful tract of land lately put on the market at very desirable rates.

The ocean view is very beautiful, as we drive along through the village of East Harwich. It is a small country place, very retired and secluded from the rest of the villages, more like the old style of Cape Cod.

38

East Harwich boasts of a very fine water front, about two and one-half miles from the village proper. The bathing beach is very fine. There is also an abundance of good fishing here.

A few miles further on we see a very large building near the water front. We find, on making inquiries, that this is the big Chatham Hotel, built by a syndicate of rich Boston capitalists, and costing over two hundred thousand dollars; but, owing to the misarrangement in selecting the location, it never paid, and after three years of loss it was sold to the Messrs. Eldridge for about fifteen thousand dollars, — not really the cost of the furniture in the building.

Mr. Eldridge is a native of Chatham, and has an elegant summer home here; and now he has built a hotel called the "Dill House," which is furnished with the elegant furniture of the once beautiful Hotel Chatham.

Water View from Residence of Hon. Marcellus Eldridge, Chatham.

Residence of Hon. Marcellus Eldridge, Chatham.

Interior of the Library of Hon. Marcellus Eldridge's Summer Home, Chatham.

41

Eldridge Library, Chatham.

This village is highly honored in having as a gift from this generous-hearted man a beautiful modern brick library, very commodious, with beautifully laid-out grounds. Near this village are situated the famous Chatham Lights, and the ocean view is unsurpassed. Many are the summer residents who come to this beautiful seashore place to spend the warm months of the year. Its streets are kept in perfect repair, and no section of the Cape has improved more in twenty years than Chatham. It has four hotels, besides many private boarding-places, and has a large number of handsome summer residences.

Chatham Light.

Interior View of Eldridge Public Library, Chatham.

The traveling men find the Ocean House the exact place to get good food, and to obtain a good clean place to rest. They also find Captain Berry, the proprietor, always in a genial mood; and they can say, after a night's rest in Chatham, that really this is the place for refreshment.

In the morning our team is brought to the door; we jump in and take a ride through the village on our way to South Chatham, which is a quiet country place, with neat houses, that have a good home look. Next comes South Harwich. Here we find another of our country villages, where the neighbors have lived in the same houses for years, many of them hardly ever leaving their native places until they are called to render up their account to Him who gave them life.

Residence of Hon. Marcellus Eldridge, Chatham.

Driving on a pleasant street, passing by nicely kept places, we come to Harwichport. Here there are many very handsome summer cottages near the water that have been built within a few years, also a good many beautiful houses built and owned by wealthy retired sea captains, for in no place in the world have there been so many sea captains raised as on Cape Cod. Many of them, having sailed to all the foreign countries where navigation has been made possible, have returned to their native birthplace to enjoy their declining years and well-earned wealth and rest.

View at Harwichport.

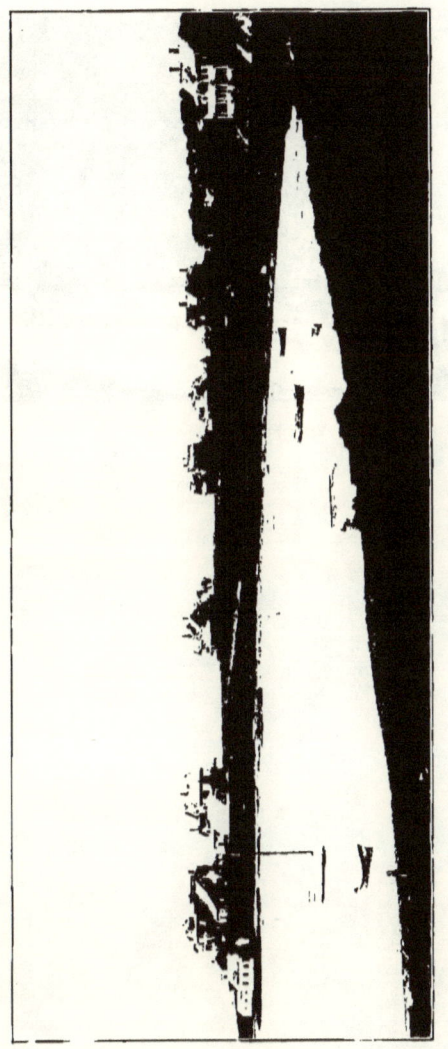

View at Harwichport.

View at Harwichport.

48

Grant Hotel, Harwichport.

The streets here are laid out very tastefully, and we shall put up for the night at the Grant House, as we have stopped in the beautiful quiet village too many times to drive by without stopping one night. We have not forgotten Mrs. Ellis's nice dinners, nor the nice warm muffins she

49

Residence of the Hon. A. N. Nickerson, Harwichport.

Residence of the Hon. Emalous Small, Harwichport.

View at Harwichport.

always has for breakfast. After having spent a pleasant night here, we start again and drive to Harwich, the same style of place as in Harwichport, — a very handsome and thrifty village, houses large, and grounds laid out in good order, fine streets shaded by beautiful trees ; and in going a few miles we come to North Harwich, a small village much like the more ancient Cape Cod.

Exchange Building, Harwich.

Harwich Center, looking South, showing Harwichport in the Distance.

53

Harwich Center, looking Southeast.

Harwich Center, looking Southwest.

From here we drive to Dennisport, and from there to Dennis, and we find a good many improvements in the way of new houses being built all along this morning's drive, which we enjoy very much. Keeping on to West Dennis, we find one of Cape Cod's richest villages, as well as a perfect nest of sea captains, with their fair daughters and handsome estates. The streets, shaded by fine trees, are well kept, splendid for driving.

View at West Harwich.

Hotel Belmont, West Harwich.

Street View at West Harwich.

I would like to take the city dude on this Cape trip with me. He
would say, long before he arrived in Boston again, that he has been surprised in finding Cape Cod what it is. As much as we enjoy some of our
suburban towns near Boston, many towns on Cape Cod lay them in the
shade for natural beauty and elegant estates. We stop here over night
at our genial friend Captain Crowell's, and have a good dinner and a
very comfortable bed where we can enjoy a good night's rest after the
long drive of the day.

We start again the next morning and drive to Yarmouth, through
East Yarmouth. Fine indeed are the beautiful houses and well-kept streets,
and from here to Hyannis one finds continual enjoyment in looking at
these fine country places.

Only a short drive from West Dennis and we come to South Dennis,
where we find some elegant residences, nearly all owned by sea captains.

Barney Gould, Residence.

At last we arrive in Hyannis, which is quite a lively town. The stores have fine plate-glass windows, there is a well-regulated bank, and it is here the new Training School and the new State Normal School are situated. This is going to be one of Cape Cod's greatest summer places.

After taking dinner at the Ivanhoe House, we drive through this village to Hyannisport, and again we look out on old ocean, and nothing looks so inviting in the summer as the open sea. Generally, we can see here all kinds of vessels, the big steamship, ploughing along on her trip

Training School, Hyannis.

Normal School, Hyannis.

New Yacht Club House, Hyannis.

59

Street View, Hyannis.

to foreign shores, the four-master, the great merchant vessels of the day, the three-masted vessels, all sizes and kinds of pleasure yachts, little cat-rigged boats and many new small sail and row boats.

The Casino, Hyannis.

Union Church, Hyannis.

Hyannisport.

Hyannisport is a very beautiful place situated on a high elevation of land, overlooking the Sound. From here we drive for about five miles and come to Craigville, another summer place lately much talked about for its delightful beach for bathing, its good boating, and cool and refreshing sea-breeze. This village is surrounded by pine trees, and is a very healthful summer place.

Shore View, Hyannis.

Residence of J. C. Clark, Hyannisport, Mass.

Leaving here our next stop is Centreville. This is the home of the Mr. Marston of the famous restaurant of that name in Boston. He was a Cape Cod boy. Some of the largest business houses in Boston to-day are run by Cape Cod boys. Take courage, boys of the Cape, be true to your homes, never forget your father's and mother's advice and counsel, and be always truthful and keep yourself pure and clean. Be careful now in your school days to improve all your time, and if you have a hasty disposition subdue it. With patience and God's care and guidance, you can do much to make for yourself a name among your friends as being a devoted son, and perhaps, sometime, yourself a kind husband and a noble father to your little ones.

Residence of Hon. Russell Marston, Centerville.

Residence of Mr. Howard Marston, Centerville.

We drive our horses into Mr. Crosby's stable, for we would not be guilty of going through this village and not stopping. We take our grip and go over to Mr. Gorham Crosby's; here we get dinner and spend the night. Such a dinner as they always had on Sunday; such biscuits, everything cooked just as nice as at Young's Hotel in Boston, and it seemed as if Mrs. Crosby could never do enough for you. Such a clean and wholesome place to sleep in, and then in the evening to sit down and have a game of checkers or dominoes, and to have some of the neighbors come in and sing, and eat apples. It was, indeed, solid rest after the long drive of the day. Really, sometimes I think I used to dread leaving such a pleasant place.

Residence of Mr. Aaron S. Crosby, Centerville.

67

Residence of Gorham F. Crosby, Centerville.

Bright and early the next day we start for Osterville, another of Cape Cod's very fashionable summer places. We find here, down on the point, a fine large hotel, but not large enough to take all who wish to come to this beautiful place. The cottages near the hotel are of the best class and the hotel guests are people who do not mind a large price, for they are, as a whole, wealthy people.

Cotocheset Hotel, Osterville.

Hotel at Osterville.

We pass through this beautiful village and come to Marston's Mills. It is a little settlement in the valley bewteen high hills, a neat and retired country village. Next we drive to Cotuit where we find another colony of retired sea captains of which Cape Cod is so proud. Here there is a delightful bay, and some very handsome and fashionable places, two large hotels, besides many private boarding houses. A very tidy place with several fine stores, and a delightful place to spend the summer. We stop over night at Captain Hallett's. The genial old Captain is always witty and good company, and his wife, like most of the other ladies on the Cape, is an extra good cook. Nowhere on the face of the earth have I ever seen such good wholesome cooking as you get on Cape Cod.

In the morning we drive to Mashpee. Here they have a hotel which can boast of having entertained General Benjamin Butler, Governor Russell, President Cleveland, Joseph Jefferson, and many other noted men. There are some of the finest ponds for trout, perch and pickerel fishing that can be found anywhere near this neat little village. The inhabitants are industrious and a peace-abiding people. They have a good school and town hall and pay strict attention to keeping the Sabbath.

It is a very beautiful drive from here through the woods to Waquoit, where we find a little bay called Waquoit Bay. The village is very neat, houses are very nicely painted. The Tobey House stands in the center of the village, its guests are always welcome. We can always find food cooked to entice the poorest appetite. So inviting is everything, one does not mind if a storm or other bad weather keeps us in doors for a few days. Governor Russell and other distinguished statesmen have been entertained here ; many very wealthy doctors, lawyers and judges come here for rest and retirement. The trout fishing and fox hunting are unsurpassed in their respective seasons.

After spending the night here, we drive through a charming country seven miles to Falmouth. The first village on our route is East Falmouth,

71

Tobey House, Waquoit, the Huntsman's Paradise.

Residence of Mr. Ignatius Sargent, Waquoit.

The Old Mill at East Falmouth.

Residence of Barzillai C. Cahoon, East Falmouth.

and we much enjoy our drive. Further on we come to Teaticket. Here we all want to stop and partake of a good dinner at Mrs. Joseph Fish's, where many of the traveling men make their headquarters. They stop here several days, and go from here to different places to return at night. Then we visit the Heights, and find a delightful summer place with old ocean in all its grandeur before us. In the distance we can see Cottage City, and Gay Head, while constantly passing are hundreds of all kinds of sailing vessels. There are many summer cottages here, which are in great demand each season.

School at Teaticket.

Morse's Pond, Falmouth.

Tower's Hotel, Falmouth Heights.

Steamer Nantucket.

Draper's Hotel, Falmouth Heights.

Following along the beach road, we see why this location is so much sought after, it is more than beautiful! Falmouth is perfectly enchanting, with its elegant mansions and streets, its fine sidewalks, and beautiful trees!

Fresh Pond, Wells' Cottages, Falmouth.

Residence of Mrs. Franklin Weld, Falmouth.

Just stop and see that elegant high school building, that fine town hall. Everything denotes thrift and advancement. Notice that elegant

The Lawrence High School, Falmouth.

Summer Residence, J. Arthur Beebe, Falmouth.

Town Hall, Falmouth.

church. It was a gift to the town from one of its rich men, Mr. Beebe. The lot alone cost fifteen thousand dollars, to say nothing about the stone church, rectory, and sheds for horses. Nothing has been left undone, no city has better-kept grounds or a finer place in which to worship. It seems to me it must be such a sweet comfort for any man to give such a

St. Barnabas Memorial Church, Falmouth.

gift as this beautiful church, or to give any other grand building that is going to be a benefit to a town or city. May its donor live long to enjoy seeing this beautiful structure standing, as it does, so magnificently speaking of the kindness of his heart. It is in this fairy garden of loveliness that the secretary of state, Richard Olney, has his summer residence, which is a mansion.

Summer Residence of Richard Olney, Sec. of State, Falmouth.

We can't find words to entirely describe the most beautiful of places. Falmouth excels all else on Cape Cod. As we drive through the streets we note the fine sidewalks, and pass many fine turnouts. One would really think we were in Newport among the Astors and Vanderbilts. We drive a few miles by some of Boston, Brooklyn and Chicago's richest men's residences; over a beautiful road from Falmouth to Quissett, our next stopping place. Now we find the most delightful harbor and grand hotels, surrounded by fine estates and well-arranged mansions. Can it be possible this is old Cape Cod ? No, it is the Cape Cod of to-day, and Falmouth, the Golden Garden City. The old hills used to sell for five dollars per acre, and the new hills now sell for two thousand dollars per acre. All this inside of twenty years.

Summer Residence of James G. Marshall, overlooking Quissett Harbor and Buzzards Bay.

Main Street, Falmouth.

Shiverick Pond, Falmouth.

Congregational Church, Falmouth.

Old Hewins Estate, Falmouth.

Quissett Harbor.

Quissett House at Quissett Harbor.

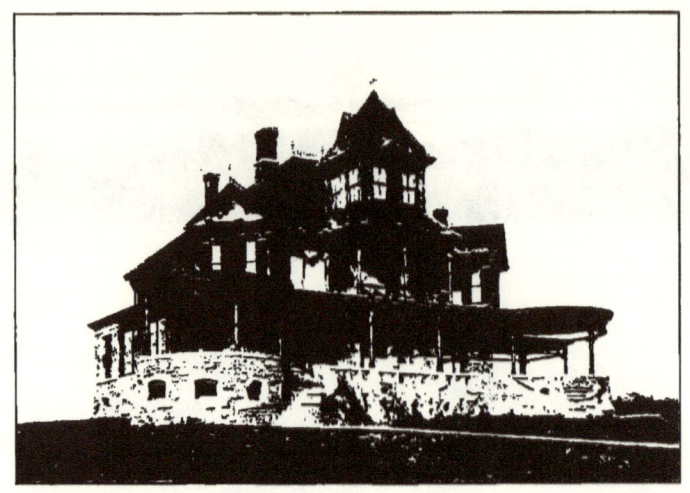

One of Quissett's Summer Residences.

We drive along to Woods Holl and are enchanted with its wonderful beauty, its many expensive and handsome estates. Here we find at the terminus of the land a beautiful village with two hotels, and always a fine, cool breeze coming from the water — Vineyard Sound on one side Buzzards Bay on the other. We can take the steamer here for New Bedford, Cottage City or Nantucket.

Church of the Messiah, Woods Holl.

Headquarters U. S. Fish Commission, Woods Holl.

Laboratory and Fish Hatching House, U. S. Commission, Woods Holl.

Beach at Penzance.

Returning to Falmouth, we keep in sight, all the time, of beautiful Buzzards Bay which is one of the very choicest bays in Massachusetts. Out a little ways from the shore we can see the lightship, called the Hen and Chickens. We watch the beautiful steam yacht owned by Mr. Benedict proudly moving up the now famous bay with some of the most distinguished men of our nation on board, going to their summer residences. The distinguished President of the United States, Grover Cleveland, is bound up the bay twenty miles to his summer home, Gray Gables.

Entering Buzzards Bay.

Nobska Light.

Leaving the village center, we find the street which leads to the next
village in the same well-kept condition, and when nearing West Falmouth
we have the bay full in view. You see in the distance Chocequoit Island.
Five years ago there was not one house on it.

West Falmouth, Chocequoit Island.

An enterprising gentleman from Boston saw its very attractive location, and invested money on that island and then began to interest his friends. He went to the town meeting at Falmouth and asked that a bridge might be put from the mainland to the island. The town refused to do it. This gentleman then laid his own plans. He went again to the town meeting and asked that he might have a road laid out with this bridge; it would cost about $3500. The town again refused; then he said that if they would lay out this road, he would guarantee in less than one year to have on the island one hundred thousand dollars' worth of taxable property and, if he did not, he would sign a bond to pay for the construction of the road and bridge, himself, endorsed by moneyed men. The road and bridge were built, and in less than the year there was $150,000 worth of taxable property for the town on this island. It has been increasing, and to-day it stands boldly as a monument to the energetic man who had pluck and endurance to carry out his good plans.

Library at West Falmouth.

Residence of Capt. Caleb O. Hamblin, West Falmouth.

Residence of Mr. Timothy Bourne, West Falmouth.

West Falmouth can boast of some very handsome and expensive summer residences. One of the most conspicuous you see, when passing on the train, is the residence of Henry Kingman of Brockton. The natives also have some very beautiful places, and fine farms. There are right here many fine lots still left to purchase, and some that there is money to be made on. We stop and take dinner with the very genial station agent, Silas Swift, and his amiable wife, as we know by experience that this is a good place. As this is the next village to Falmouth, they are at work, as in the sister village, fast improving all their estates, and are gradually and proudly advancing to be a banner village, and a very progressive one.

Summer Residence of Hon. Henry M. Kingman, West Falmouth.

Old Landmark at West Falmouth,
Owned by Silas Swift.

Old Davis Farm, West Falmouth.

Now our route is along the beautiful country roads. A great change has been made since the railroad was built, twenty years ago. All the people used to travel on the old stagecoach, run by Mr. Hewens for years; now they use the railroad. Compare the places then, to the well-kept, up-to-date estates of to-day. There is a wonderful change for the better. We come to the fine estate of Dr. Miller, a New York man, who has

Residence of Dr. Chas. S. Miller, North Falmouth.

everything necessary to make life happy, being a retired gentleman who came to this quiet village to pass his declining years on his fine farm, which each year he makes more beautiful. This has got to be quite a Miller neighborhood, as the doctor owns several fine places adjoining his estate.

Now we drive along to North Falmouth, and notice, just before entering the village, a sign-board "Wild Harbor." Turning down this delightful country drive, we reach the bay, Wild Harbor, we find nine

Residence of Downer Bros., Wild Harbor.

Residence of Downer Bros., Wild Harbor.

well arranged and well furnished cottages, owned by the Downer Brothers of Boston, two of which have been occupied by them for years. These beautiful places were built for their own convenience and, seeing the benefit they and their families received, they decided to build more cottages, which they lease each year. The whole grounds show exquisite taste and refinement.

Residences of Downer Bros., Wild Harbor.

Returning to the village of North Falmouth, we find a little settlement, the houses neatly and prettily arranged, well cared for, and up to
date. On our drive, we see a guideboard marked '' Megansett.'' Driving
down there, we find Hon. Frank Nye's new, fashionable Megansett, with
its fine summer houses. This was a few years ago a cow-pasture, and at
that time only valued at about five dollars per acre. Now it is held at a
high price.

Home of Hon. Francis Nye, North Falmouth.

Hon. Francis Nye.

Snapshot of Megansett.

Residence of Dr. Donkins, North Falmouth, "Cedar Crest."

We drive along, and soon come to Cataumet. Here we find a quiet country village, with some fine farms and well-kept houses owned by some of our honored and retired sea captains. We come to another guideboard, and it reads "Scraggy Neck" and "Cataumet Depot." After passing under the railroad tracks, we come to the Jochim Cottage, owned for twenty-four years by our esteemed townsman, Mr. Alden P. Davis. Many noted men come here for rest and retirement because they are so highly entertained and well provided for.

ISLAND HAVEN,

SUMMER RESIDENCE OF

THOS. A. BAXENDALE,

AMRITA ISLAND, CATAUMET.

Amrita Island is only fifteen minutes' walk from Cataumet Station. Springs of purest water abound, trickling down the grassy bluffs, making this one of Nature's own delightful summer resorts.

The lover of aquatic sports finds his paradise right here, as the water abounds in fish of all descriptions. The bathing is luxurious, as the warm waves leap on the white sanded shore of the sheltered Squeteague Bay, making this an unusually attractive place.

Summer Residence of Hon. Thos. A. Baxendale, Amrita Island, Cataumet.

We drive by some of the best estates on Cape Cod, with a beautiful water view all the way, and do not wonder that people come to this much favored place, Scraggy Neck. This little point of land was at one time owned and occupied by the late Capt. Charles Parker; when he bought it, and gave one thousand dollars for it, we thought that a great price. Now it is owned by Mr. Eustis, one of Dorchester's richest men, and the house which is being built for Mr. Eustis, by Mr. M. C. Waterhouse of Bourne is to cost one hundred thousand dollars. Here we have one of the most magnificent views of the bay, a natural harbor and a splendid bathing beach.

Residence of the Hon. D. D. Nye, Cataumet.

Bay View House, Fred Dimmock Prop., Cataumet.

On our trip, we pass through the remainder of the village of Cataumet, till we come to the old mill near the famous Red Brook House.
Here we find some very fine summer houses. One lately added to the
number is the elegant residence of Mr. Wm. Power Wilson, which has a
very commanding view of the bay. We can overlook the Taunton Club
grounds, a beautiful tract of land, and we think, " How kindly nature has
dealt with us, for there is no place on our ride where the natural scenery
and the splendid country views intermingle with the water views as it
does along our Buzzards Bay."

Residence of Walter H. Wing, Cataumet.

As we pass some well-kept farms, you might ask, "Can anyone raise anything on Cape Cod?" And I will answer, "Beautiful crops of vegetation are here raised and always sold at good advantage, for the demand is greater than the supply, and the price realized always proves that it is time well spent in having a good big garden." Now we find ourselves in the most lovely little village of Pocasset, or (as we call it)

Residence of Mrs. Wester, Pocasset.

Estate of the late Capt. Jos. Dimmock, Pocasset.

Residence of Mrs. Brackett, Pocasset.

Residence of T. F. Cook, Pocasset.

Residence of George Kendrick, Pocasset.

Barlow Town, on account of so many of that name who live here. It is an ideal little village, and the stranger always delights to take a ride through here. Some of Boston's business men, who first came from the city for rest and the reviving of their health, found it to be better than medicine. The air was so balmy and invigorating that they finally built for themselves fine places. Here the well-known Professor Wood of Harvard has his summer residence, and across on the North Shore we see many cottages that have been built the last few years. They, too, have a fine view of Buzzards Bay. We take the four-mile drive to Wing's Neck, as it is called, where there is a lighthouse that has been cared for by the same family for more than forty years.

Summer Residence of Prof. E. S. Wood, Pocasset.

Dining Room of Prof. E. S. Wood's Summer House, Pocasset.

Wing's Neck Light, Buzzards Bay.

Residence and Store of Asa Raymond, Pocasset.

M. E. Chapel, Pocasset.

Residence of Dr. Babcock, Pocasset.

Returning, and passing many pretty homes, we come to the turn of
the road leading to Bourne. If we cared to drive from this point directly
northeast, we would come to a very beautiful pond called Snake Pond.
There are many other handsome ponds near this secluded little village,
which is called Forestdale — a perfect name for the place. It is right in

Snake Pond, Forestdale.

the forest, but the people are very pleasant and their houses very neat. At the junction of the road we see a very handsome place, owned by our much esteemed friend, the Hon. William Blackwell of New York. He, having retired from active business life many years ago, built this place

Residence of Wm. R. Blackwell, Pocasset.

here for his summer home, where he enjoys good health. He has for a long time stopped here the year round. Passing a beautiful pond near this fine estate, we come to a red-roofed building, once the pride of Bourne as it was then an iron foundry and did a flourishing business. Then some of our now retired sea captains used to run cargoes from here to New York. Now it belongs to the Tobey Island Club.

Residence of Wm. R. Blackwell, Pond View, Pocasset.

Driving on, passing several village homes, we arrive at a crossroad, and on the guideboard we read "Monument Beach." Down this road, we see on the left an old landmark, the homes of Mr. Silas Perry and Capt. George E. Phinney, and on the right the very handsome cottage of Capt. S. Henry Perry, who commands one of the finest new three-masters on our coast.

Next we come to the cottage of one of our schoolmates, J. F. Perry, who is one of the best yachtsmen on the bay. Then to the estate of Dr. Leonard Latter, who is a fine gentleman and a very talented and skillful physician, one who never hesitates in his calls to duty, no matter how adverse the circumstances.

Across the way is the fine estate of Capt. E. H. Tobey, who after following the sea for years has returned to his birthplace to enjoy the remainder of his life with his family and friends.

Looking West, Monument Beach Road.

Summer Residence of Mr. Levi D. Brown, Monument Beach.

Union Chapel, Monument Beach.

Residence of Mr. Charles Cook, Monument Beach.

Residence of W. W. Phinney, Monument Beach.

Residence of Wm. E. C. Perry, Monument Beach.

Residence and Studio of Mrs. M. C. Allen, Monument Beach.

Residence of R. M. Perry, Monument Beach.

At Monument Beach we find quite a settlement of summer houses and a post-office. The water view is unsurpassed. There are two hotels, "The Monument Beach House," and the "Norcross House," the latter being one of the very best arranged hotels on the Cape, and there is not another hotel that has such a beautiful location, standing as it does, nearly on the water's edge, with verandas on three stories and on all sides. It is arranged with open plumbing, and the sanitary conditions are the best. It has every convenience found in a first-class hotel. Here there is a sea wall, costing thousands of dollars, which is the finest piece of stone work that has ever been laid on Cape Cod.

Norcross House, Monument Beach.

Looking North from Norcross House, Monument Beach.

129

Monument Beach View.

One of the best views of Buzzards Bay is at the summer home of Mr. Ambert Howard, standing as it does on a high elevation overlooking the bay for miles and the beautiful country along the shore. This house has lately been remodeled and is an honor to the village.

Next to this stands the fine summer home of Mr. Nichols.

On the Green, Monument Beach.

Boating and bathing are excellent. Excursion steamers come from all points. The cottages that are being built of late are of newer style of architecture, and many of the old ones are being remodeled. Monument Beach can boast of several millionaires who reside here during the summer season, and the class of people that come here is the best. It makes this little village appear quite like a large town when our city friends are here for the summer.

Steamer Gay Head.

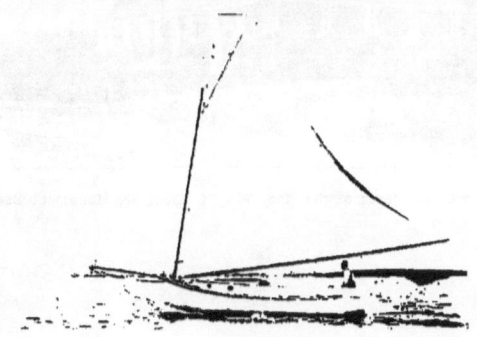

Cat Boat Mona.

Take a good look at our own little town of Bourne which has been a township only twelve years. We find the assessed property last year was $1,709,775, and the increase of valuation in 1894 was $42,300. Number of new residents assessed, 329; residents, 466. Certainly a good showing for so small a place. On the beach, we find many handsome estates. The ones of especial interest are the new houses of Hon. William L. Douglas

Summer Residence of the Hon. Wm. L. Douglas, Monument Beach.

of Brockton, who has just completed a magnificent residence, and the grand estate of Mr. Fred Packard, which overlooks the bay and country for miles. While others are very fine, none on Cape Cod go ahead of this place for its natural beauty and views.

And from the spring house to the hotel on both sides of the street are some of our handsomest summer homes. They command the very best water views on the beach, and are owned by wealthy people who have been here for years to enjoy the beauties of Buzzards Bay.

Summer Residence of Mr. Fred Packard, Monument Beach.

See what an elegant mansion Mr. George Gardner has. One can hardly believe there could be such a delightful place. And the Bungalow built by Mr. Gardner, Sr., eclipses anything else around here, with its perfect

House of Mr. George Gardner, Jr., Monument Beach.

"The Bungalow," Summer Residence of Mr. George Gardner, Sr., Monument Beach.

water privileges. There is the Tobey Island House on the island that used to be owned by my father, and was sold, like much of our property, for a small sum of money. I believe it was less than $200. Afterwards it was sold for $1,000, and when it brought that price it was considered enormous. And now Judge Gray of Boston, one of the club members, sitting on the veranda of the clubhouse, said he did not think they would sell one end of the island for $75,000. Only think of it; my father got $200 for it. Well, we are living on the new Cape Cod, or perhaps I should say the progressive Cape Cod. We did not then have the President of the United States, statesmen, congressmen, doctors, lawyers, bankers, and millionaires by the hundreds for neighbors, as we do to-day. Cape Cod is destined to be one of the greatest watering-places this globe has ever seen. We have only begun in our advancement. Time will do as much in the next twenty years as it has in the past.

We take the rest of our drive over the beach road to Bourne village, passing a fine estate owned by Capt. Abraham Phinney, the Captain being one of our oldest townsmen. He has always been a hard-working man; and now in his declining years, he is taking his well-earned rest.

Residence of Capt. Abraham Phinney, Monument Beach.

We now come to the home of an old schoolmate, Chas. H. Phinney, and in our memory still lingers the many pleasant evenings spent here in our childhood's days.

Next we come to an old estate once owned by Grandpa Phinney, as we used to call him. He was one of those men who wanted good use made of everything. One day when I was about ten years of age, I was up near his house playing with other boys. The old gentleman in taking out his wallet to pay the butcher lost ten dollars, the wind blowing it away. We boys heard the old man scream when he saw his money going. We saw it go into the air, but did not see it come down. He was very much excited, and said, "Boys, the one who finds my money shall have some apples to eat." We commenced to hunt for it, and after a while I found it. I gave it to the old man and he looked at me and said, "Well, boy, I said you should have some apples, but you are eating apples now and you do not deserve any more." It seems to me that now I can almost hear the shout of the other boys. At that we walked away, but had not gone far when the old gentleman's wife appeared at the other side of the house. She had seen all the fuss, and told me to undo my shirt waist, and she just filled it out with apples so that I could hardly walk. I guess she was pretty well acquainted with the old man's ways herself.

Summer Residence of Mrs. E. B. Phinney, Monument Beach.

137

We pass along and come to a very neat little cottage house where reside Captain and Mrs. Phinney, and the next cottage looks so nice to us, we linger along to see its well-kept lawn. Soon we come to

Residences of Capt. Jesse F. Phinney and Mr. Henry Chester, Monument Beach.

Boat Shop of W. W. Phinney, Monument Beach.

the woods where a few years ago it used to be a lonely walk ; now we see some very neat houses, then pass the home of Grandma Bailey (as we used to call her). We can never forget the many kind acts done by her for us.

Residence of the late Josiah Bailey, Monument Beach

We ride past the little village school, the training place of boys and girls in the town for generations back. The land was given to the town by my grandfather for a schoolhouse lot. Later on, one-half acre was given in addition by a near neighbor.

Village School, Monument Beach.

Across the way is the oldest estate in the town of Bourne. One of those old places that have always been kept up and well preserved, with its graded lawn, it looks, in its perfect neatness, as it did when I was a small boy. It is very attractive, and much admired by everyone. It is owned by the oldest man in the town, one who has followed the sea for years and has always been successful. To-day there are not many men of sixty who can endure more work or who have a more erect carriage in walking than Captain Burgess has at eighty.

Residence of Capt. S. S. Burgess, Monument Beach.

Norman E. Perry.

A small cottage house across the way is the home of the writer of this Trip around Cape Cod, and everything connected with the place is enshrined in my heart. Its old stone walls, each tree, and every inch of land has a memory dear to me. Although we have lived in better places, still how natural for us Americans to sing, "Be it ever so humble, there's no place like home." I find it very inviting to enter my own home and see my wife and my dear little boy, but I will only stop now for a few moments.

Old Homestead of E. G. Parry, Monument Beach.

After taking our trip around the Cape, we find as many changes in Bourne as anywhere. Nearly all the dear old familiar faces of childhood's days have gone from our gaze, but not from our hearts; and we hope we may be the means of doing some kindness to others, so at last, when we are laid away, we, too, may be remembered.

We continue on down the street, and if any of the stones along this road were misplaced, I think I would know it. It is a part of my history. I love to see the old fences and stone walls; they are my childhood's friends. We pass along a well-kept street, and nearly all the houses for a few miles are the same familiar places of yore. Occasionally we find an alteration.

Residence of Capt. Samuel Bourne, Monument Beach.

Then go over to the brook. How we always enjoyed looking at this stream of water. It is one of the sweetest recollections of my childhood days. In this brook we used to play by the hour with our pants turned up, wading, and making mud ponds, catching polywogs, putting them in again, and sailing boats. We remember a little, lame old man — a kind old gentleman — who used to sit out of doors near by and watch us. His house has been purchased by our distinguished friend, C. F. Chamberlayne, who was one of our Cape Cod boys, and now a lawyer of some fame. This is his summer residence.

Residence of C. F. Chamberlayne, Monument Beach.

Next came the old mill; in my childhood days, I used to go down there sometimes on Saturday to spend the afternoon and see my old friend, Mr. Bailey, grind the corn into meal. He used to let us boys play tag and such games, and we had fun. Well, the old mill is gone, but children's memories revive the old scenes. All along the road at nearly every house, we see in our minds dear departed friends, their kind and loving faces we will ever hold dear in our memories.

Next to where the old mill stood stands the house now occupied by D. W. O. Ellis and the Rev. Nathan N. Chamberlayne, a retired Episcopal divine, a man of great learning and a thorough student. We understand that the reverend gentleman has one of the largest libraries in town. He is quite extensively engaged in the raising of cranberries, and pays out a good many hundreds of dollars each year to our village people. His house is one of the old landmarks.

Cranberry Scene.

One old familiar landmark is the Sherman Ellis estate, now owned by Mr. Appleton of Boston, as his summer residence. He has made such a wonderful change in this place that I think if the old man, Mr. Ellis, was to come back to earth again, he himself would hardly know his old homestead.

Summer Residence of Mr. Geo. B. Appleton, Bourne.

The next place is owned by Mr. Benedict, and a fine place indeed has he made this. We do not realize the beautiful places we have; nature has indeed lavished its beautiful nativeness all around us, and it wants only a little money to more perfectly bring out what God has meant for his people to enjoy, the wonderful attractiveness of nature.

Summer Residence of Mr. John Benedict, Bourne, Mass.

Now we come to the home and studio of Mr. Chas. Raliegh and stop to admire the fine marine views in his store windows.

Passing the farm of Capt. Russell Blackwell, one would hardly believe such fine produce could be raised on this estate, but the Captain puts forth honest labor, and fine indeed are the crops he has raised.

M. E. Parsonage, Bourne.

Residence of Geo. I. Briggs, Bourne.

Now we come to the noted Monument Neck famed as the summer residence of President Cleveland. Down this road, we will just take a peep at Gray Gables. The land a few years ago could have been bought for four dollars per acre; now money cannot buy it. Near Gray Gables are the Williams, the Appletons, the Hardys and the Parkersons. They all own exceptionally handsome residences, with many acres of land around them. Returning, we notice there are many fine country residences all along, and near the junction of the road is our own familiar parsonage. Just a little way toward Bourne lives a lady whom I always love to speak to. She was, in my earliest childhood days, my Sabbath-school teacher, and I always think of her with love and good wishes for her faithfulness to the little boys entrusted to her care. We now come to our church, the M. E. Church in Bourne. Here the people are to be

M. E. Church, Bourne.

found on Sunday, and I think I can say with pride Bourne people are very generous. They are willing to sustain the church and every good and charitable cause. Near the church is a new and very handsome public library donated to the town by Miss Bourne of New Bedford, in honor of the memory of her father, once a country boy. The old name of Monument was changed to Bourne in honor of this man.

New Library at Bourne.

Grammar School, Bourne.

The gift of the library was a blessing to the town. It is a beautiful building, built of fancy brick, and cost twenty thousand dollars. May joy and sweet rest be to the donor. A little further on, after we leave the church, we come to the familiar house of one of our most respected citizens, Hon. Albert Eldridge, and his beautiful house is an honor to our town. We look with pride, also, on his brother Frank's house, across the way. We must admit our country boys are up to the times.

Turning the corner, we find some houses which are old landmarks, and a fine new house built by our genial friend, Mr. Daggett. Driving

Looking South at Bourne Corners.

Residence of M. C. Waterhouse, Bourne.

down to the depot we first come to our Town Clerk's house, which always looks trim and well kept ; next is our "Welcome Hall," for all things that are good are welcome in Bourne ; finally, we come to and cross the bridge over Monument River. Here the old landmarks are all gone, for we have a new depot, two new stores, lumber yards, and a busy thoroughfare instead.

Welcome Hall, Bourne.

View at Bourne Station.

Residence of A. F. Swift, Bourne.

Dear reader, I have given you a long ride around Cape Cod. It has taken us about two weeks. The horses are tired and need rest, and so for a few days we will stop in Bourne before finishing our drive around the upper end and westerly shore of Buzzards Bay. Driving to my home my loved ones are all glad to see me back again.

Now we are ready to start again. Leaving Bourne Station, and passing some very finely kept places, we soon come to the old Bourne House, built in 1662, and now owned and occupied by Capt. Henry Bourne, of New York, who spends his summers at this fine old

Residence of Capt. Henry Bourne, Bourne.

place. We drive along, and soon come to the home of one of our old school teachers, a lady whom we are always pleased to see. At the corner we could take the road to Buzzards Bay, but we go straight on, passing the estate of one of our Bourne boys, Mr. Jerome L. Bourne, nephew of the late Jonathan Bourne of New Bedford. As we drive by we notice the great improvements which have been made by the Puritan Club, a very rich class of Boston's retired business men, who have built a beautiful clubhouse on a high bluff, near one of our lakes, overlooking the surrounding country.

Near by is the fine estate of the Manomet Club, and we find, on looking up the history of this Club, that it is one of the oldest, if not the oldest, and richest on Cape Cod. The grounds are always well kept, and everything is in apple-pie order. Next we come to the old home of M. C. Waterhouse, a most beautiful place, now owned by Mr. Horton. We drive by some beautiful places, and are nearly opposite the estate of

Summer Residence of Rev. W. V. Morrison, Buzzards Bay.

Joseph Jefferson, on Buttermilk Bay, past the little schoolhouse on the hill, and then to the home of the Rev. Mr. Morrison. Here is a very fine view of the bay and the surrounding country. The reverend gentleman is very extensively engaged in raising cranberries. He has laid out thousands of dollars, and we trust he will soon realize a good profit on the money invested. Mr. Morrison had the honor of being the school teacher of the President of the United States, William McKinley, in his boyhood days. We drive along, and come to the home of Mr. Stillman Ryder. Many are the traveling men who have been entertained at this hospitable home in the days gone by.

From here we drive towards Wareham ; and I must tell you a little story about an old gentleman, a native of the Cape, who last year was so shocked by one of those dashing new women jumping off her wheel before his team, and exclaiming, "Is this the way to Wareham ?" The old gentleman, being a little deaf, did not quite understand her meaning, and looking at her for one moment answered, "Some wear 'em that way and some don't ; but if you want to go to Wareham, keep along up this road two miles and you will find it." No wonder the old gentleman was shocked when he looked at the object before him. It was his first sight of bloomers, and I do not wonder at his amazement on looking at the new woman for the first time. I think it is a grand exercise to ride a wheel as a lady should ride one, but I think it is detestable when a lady dresses herself up in male attire. We love to think of a lady as modest and refined, as kind, gentle and womanlike, as an adornment to society, but it takes all those finer feelings from our minds if we think the young ladies are all going to follow in the footsteps of the new woman.

Driving along, the next place we come to is Point Independence, which overlooks Buzzards Bay. Here we find great improvements. Many fine and very handsome estates are being built here each year. We cross the bridge and find ourselves in Onset. Here nature has lav-

Residence of Edw. N. Pigot, Buzzards Bay.

ished some of its richest gifts on this beautiful little Onset Bay. Many are the elegant houses here, and lots of new ones are added each year. On the point called Wareham Point there are some of the finest estates that we have on our whole coast, while just a little way below here we come to a point of land called Tempest Knob, where there are some of the handsomest places with well-kept grounds, owned by rich summer residents. Driving through Onset, East Wareham is reached, a quiet little country village, next to Wareham. This is the center to which many of the Cape ladies are wont to come and do their shopping. Here we find well-arranged stores, and a wide-awake, business-like appearing place.

We drive through this very attractive town, by some beautiful estates, through well-laid-out streets, shaded by fine trees, and soon we come to Tremont. Here we find the nail works where the business of manufacturing nails has been carried on for over half a century. Passing through this village we find ourselves in Marion. This is one of the ban-

View at Onset.

Point Independence, Onset.

ner villages of Buzzards Bay. At Onset, we find an ideal summer location. In looking down the Bay from the high bluff, we see several islands, most prominent among them is Wicket Island, Little Bird Island, Little Harbor, Little Pine, Barrows and Scraggy Islands, and from these islands are several inlets. This is one of the most delightful places on Buzzards Bay for boating. Near by are many fresh water ponds where excellent fishing is much enjoyed by such noted men as ex-President Cleveland and Joe Jefferson. The salt water fishing about Onset is also of the best. From

Residence of James Baker, Onset.

The Temple at Onset, Mass.

Onset we find a very attractive drive on our way to Wareham, through the village of Agawam, this village being named for an old and brave tribe of Indians who lived there two hundred years ago. Wareham, one of the oldest villages on Buzzards Bay, situated in Plymouth County, derived its name from historical Wareham in one of the English townships. The village was incorporated in 1739, and like many of our other ancestral villages, the first thought was for each settler to have an ample tract of land for his own disposal; also to have a church site and cemetery. Many were the encounters here had with the Indians, in settling the disputes over the first tracts of land. We find Wareham of to-day a beautiful country village, with a variety of stores, and a substantial bank system. Many of the residents of near-by villages find this the most convenient and best place to do their banking business, and to purchase useful articles for their homes.

Odd Fellows' Hall, Wareham.

Bank Building and Street Views, Wareham.

From Wareham we continue our drive on our way to Marion, and we find the roads in an unusually attractive condition, as they are macadamized. Marion is one of the most attractive and beautiful seashore villages on Buzzards Bay. One of its attractions is the fine and commodious hotel, the "Sippecan," with Casino connected. It is here that the summer guests have a well-arranged hotel, with wide verandas, well-furnished rooms, excellent table service; and best of all the Casino is right at the water's edge, allowing the guests to have advantages here not obtained in many other seashore hotels. We find the drives in Marion simply grand, as there are many beautiful shade trees and some of the finest estates that can be found anywhere. Here the Tabor Academy is located, a college endowed to the town. The buildings are well arranged and well kept, usually have full attendance of pupils, not only from the villages near by, but oftentimes from adjoining states. It was in this village that ex-President and Mrs. Cleveland first made their headquarters and summer home when coming to Buzzards Bay, before they purchased "Gray Gables," which is only five miles across the bay from Marion. From here we drive

The Sippecan House.

C. W. Ripley, Proprietor, Marion, Mass.

Street View, Marion.

Congregational Chapel, Marion.

Tabor Academy, Marion, Mass., Dana M. Dustan, Principal.

Summer Residence of H. R. Reed, Marion, Mass.

Ned's Point Light, Mattapoisett.

through Mattapoisett and find another of Buzzards Bay's famous seashore watering places. The country about this village is quite uneven, there being many high and commanding views, making the seashore most attractive and the drives most delightful and enjoyable. The estates in this village are of the better class, and the native village homes are well kept and well cared for. Six miles from here are the busy and attractive sister cities, Fairhaven and New Bedford, beautifully located on a prominent point of Buzzards Bay and here we finish our delightful drive around Cape Cod.

Town Hall, Mattapoisett.

The South Shore.—Although the North Shore is one of nature's own delightful summer resorts, still, for beautiful sandy beaches, excellent bathing, boating and fishing, the South Shore by far excels the North Shore. Rightfully the South Shore begins at the branch of N. Y. N. H. & H. R. R. at Braintree, one of the oldest townships in or about Boston. The town was incorporated in 1640, and was named from Braintree, England, like many other places which bear ancient names of the fatherland country. For years this town was connected with Quincy, Randolph and Holbrook, but in the year 1708 it was set off as a separate township. Many noted persons were born and raised in this old town of Braintree. John Adams, second President of the United States spent his boyhood's days here, and John Quincy Adams, sixth President of the United States was born here, also many other noted and distinguished men. Braintree is particularly noted for its extensive estates, its modern-built residences, its beautiful drives and its delightful views from the higher elevations. From Braintree we can see the Blue Hills and Cochato Rivers, which unite to form the Monatiquot River, and this empties into the Weymouth Fore River. Also there are two fine fresh water ponds originally called Gooch and Cranberry, where fish abound in goodly numbers. The next town below is Weymouth. This town was incorporated in 1635, five years before Braintree, and many Indian stories could the old inhabitants tell of encounters with the old chieftains and warriors. Many fierce battles were fought by our forefathers and earlier settlers, and it was at Weymouth that Myles Standish led his band of brave followers forth to battle. Sometimes he was met by several tribes, and history gives it that two noted chieftains, Mattawamat and Pecksuot, with many of their brave warriors were here slain by Myles Standish and his followers; but in 1676 the town was again attacked by the Indians, and many buildings burned. The Indian name of the place was Wessagusett, but the town was supposed to be named from Weymouth, England. The first settlers here were not our Pilgrim Fathers, for they were not a religious or a peace-abiding people; they were inclined to be lawless and far from doing right. The original colonists remained only a short time, and soon a better class took their places, and the latter were really the founders of the town.

There is no town on the South Shore where there are so many imposing dwellings as Weymouth, and this town can boast of having exceedingly picturesque water views. From the higher elevations it is perfectly enchanting. Being so close to Boston, Hull, Nantasket, and many other inviting summer resorts, it is no wonder this fine town is always overrun with summer tourists. The water is exceedingly fine for bathing, boating and fishing. Next town is Hingham, where we find the coast is not so evenly laid out, there being many ragged boulders all along the shore front, which the summer tourists like to see: also many inlets and small bays, making its shores wonderfully attractive for their natural nativeness, and near by we can see the Weir River with a very ragged coast.

On the highlands there are some of the most commanding views of the adjoining towns. Prospect Hill is about 250 feet above sea level and several other hills are nearly as high. There are some fine farms in Hingham, which send their produce to our Boston market. Hingham has some fine fresh water ponds like her adjoining towns, already visited. They have a fine public library, and it is in this village that the Derby Academy was endowed by Sarah Derby in 1797. And it is here that

Main Street, Hingham, from Railroad Crossing. Photographed by F. L. Temple.

Oldest Church in New England. Built in 1682. Unitarian Church, Hingham, Mass.

The John R. Brewer House, Hingham, Mass.

they have the oldest church in all New England, first used in 1682, and they have one of the finest cemeteries in Massachusetts. We see on the headstones names of many noted men there laid to rest, and it is here, in Hingham, that our Secretary of the Navy, Hon. John D. Long, has his beautiful home. Many beautiful old elm trees adorn the streets in this grand old place. The town was settled in 1633 by people of the old country, who formerly came from Hingham, England, and was incorporated in 1635. The Indians had many a bloody battle here under Phillip, and here many noted men were born. The high elevation of land, with just breeze enough from the water, makes Hingham a delightful summer place. Its streets are always well kept, and many enchanting drives here abound. It is only a few miles from here to Nantasket Beach, and many fine farms are scattered about. The drive from Hingham is very delightful, as there is just roughness enough in the natural make-up of the country to make it wonderfully attractive. Many fishermen's cottages can be seen. The roads are made to look as rustic as possible, as the old lanes and country roads have been traveled for centuries both by our old-fashioned country friends and, originally, by the Indians. Little did the country people dream it would some day be such a fine watering place as it is now.

Residence of Hon. John D. Long, Secretary of the Navy, Hingham, Mass.

Nantasket is of very narrow width, from forty to sixty feet from bay to ocean, and many are the associations connected with Nantasket as a summer resort. It surpasses all others in New England for its enchanting water views. The most renowned Minot's Ledge Lighthouse can be seen from this point, and many a mariner has thanked his Creator for the grand flash of Minot's Light when tossed about in storm and tempest. The hills that used to be unadorned, now boast of some of New England's finest summer houses. Not only do our richest people find enchantment here, but many in the humbler walks of life come down here to pass their vacation, camping out in tents here pitched by happy families for their summer outing. Countless are the fine turnouts always on the move at this fascinating seashore watering place. Pleasant, indeed, is the sight to see the bathers waiting for a big wave to roll in so they can dive under its dashing billows, and thousands are the ships of all grades and classes.

View at Nantasket Beach.   Photographed by E. A. Bartlett, Nantasket.

from the pleasure steam yacht to the transatlantic steamers plowing along to far-off lands, that can be seen here. A very short distance from Nantasket is the noted " Harding's Ledge," where there is a large bell buoy. In bad weather the mariner is ever on the alert for this warning bell. Farther out is the whistling buoy on the so-called " Graves."

Hotel Pemberton is right on the water's edge, and one can get a commanding view of the bay and the surrounding seashore resorts, and feel the delightful sea breezes. Many hills are here seen, one of the principal ones being Telegraph Hill, and history gives it that this was one of the landmarks of the Indians in the bygone days, where many battles were fought by our brave forefathers.

Another prominent location is Point Allerton, with a very high and lofty peak. Here an expensive sea-wall has been built by the United States Government, and from this location we can see many other commanding hills for which the south shore is so famous. At Hull there is one of the finest yacht club houses in Massachusetts. Returning to Nantasket, we notice some of the largest summer hotels on the whole New England coast, and nothing for water views or beautiful sandy beaches for bathing can eclipse this most wonderful location. The Hotel Nantasket, the Atlantic House and the Rockland House, are three of the most commanding and best arranged hotels on our whole seacoast. A short distance from this point, we come to the Black Rock House, and the Pacific House, situated near the much-talked-of Jerusalem Road. Fine marine views and elegant estates can be seen all along this road, reminding one of the old country.

The Oregon House, Hull, Mass.

View at Stony Beach and Point Allerton.

176

The Atlantic House, Nantasket Beach.

Rockland House, Nantasket.

177

On Jerusalem Road.

View on the Jerusalem Road.

Residence of Dr. C. B. Bridgham, Cohasset.

Some of the estates are laid out with such stately magnificence, and the foliage is so beautiful, one is apt to exclaim, " Is this our beloved New England !"

Often we see here many fine turnouts of the rich, and many less gorgeous and less pretentious turnouts of our plain country folks; still all enjoy this beautiful rustic drive. Cohasset was originally an Indian name called Connohasset, and much interest is always shown in looking at the rugged rocks and projecting cliffs seen all along through this section of our journey. The views in Cohasset are wonderfully fine, and many are the fashionable summer rusticators always found here in great numbers. Its situation is so near Boston, it makes a summer resort very convenient for business men. Beautiful as the estates are, the country is rough and rocky. Oftentimes the cliffs rise 180 to 200 feet above sea level.

Osgood's School, Cohasset.

View at Cohasset. Looking northwest from Kents Rocks.

Residence of Oliver H. Howe, M. D., Cohasset, Mass.

At Cohasset the boating and bathing are exceptionally inviting, there being so many little dotted inlets and rugged cliffs, interspersed with fine sandy benches. In going a few miles, we soon come to another watering place, which is North Scituate. Here we find some of the most magnificent seashore homes. Also fine streets, grand ocean views, and an exceptionally fine sandy beach for bathing. This is one of the most attractive sea shore resorts on the whole south shore. Then we come

View at Cohasset, looking north.

Cohasset Common.

Junction of Elm and South Main Street, looking southeast, Cohasset.

View at Cohasset, looking east from Kents Rocks.

Cohasset Yacht Club House.

View at Cohasset, looking northeast from Kents Rocks.

New Driveway, Cohasset.

View of Cohasset, from Kents Rocks, looking west.

View of Cohasset, from Kents Rocks, looking southwest.

View of North Scituate Beach, looking south.

Life-Saving Station at North Scituate.

View of North Scituate Beach, looking north.

Residence of George V. Yenetchi, Scituate.

Looking east from Cedar Point, Scituate.

The Old Scituate Light.

Looking west from Cedar Point, Scituate.

to Scituate Harbor, a trim little village of permanent residents, and a place much sought after by the summer tourists. This village is noted for its quaintness, its old-time streets and drives, and its fine sea coast ; here also we find an abandoned lighthouse. Scituate was incorporated in 1849, and in by-gone days many were the ships built from the wood cut in the near-by forests. Soon we come to Marshfield, which is noted for

View at Scituate Harbor. The First Cliff.

Street View at Scituate.

Street View, Scituate, near Four Corners.

Residence of Frank Doherty, Second Cliff, Scituate.

Homestead of the Author of the Old Oaken Bucket, Greenbush.

THE OLD OAKEN BUCKET.

" How dear to my heart are the scenes of my childhood,
    When fond recollection presents them to view!
The orchard, the meadow, the deep-tangled wildwood,
    And every loved spot which my infancy knew,
The wide-spreading pond, and the mill that stood by it,
    The bridge and the rock where the cataract fell.
The cot of my father, the dairy house nigh it,
    And e'en the rude bucket that hung in the well,
The old oaken bucket, the iron-bound bucket,
The moss-covered bucket that hung in the well.

" That moss-covered bucket I hailed as a treasure,
    For often at noon, when returned from the field,
I found it the source of an exquisite pleasure,
    The purest and sweetest that nature can yield.
How ardent I seized it, with hands that were glowing,
    And quick to the white-pebbled bottom it fell.
Then soon, with the emblem of truth overflowing,
    And dripping with coolness it rose from the well.
The old oaken bucket, the iron-bound bucket,
The moss-covered bucket arose from the well.

" How sweet from the green mossy brim to receive it,
    As, poised on the curb, it inclined to my lips!
Not a full-blushing goblet could tempt me to leave it,
    Tho' filled with the nectar that Jupiter sips.
And now, far removed from the loved habitation,
    The tear of regret will intrusively swell,
As fancy reverts to my father's plantation,
    And sighs for the bucket that hung in the well;
The old oaken bucket, the iron-bound bucket,
The moss-covered bucket which hangs in the well."—SAMUEL WOODWORTH.

Brant Rock, looking south from Life-Saving Station.

Minot's Light.

its fine farms. The Indian name of the town was Missaucatusket. We find that from here it is only a short drive to Duxbury, Pembroke, and several other villages. It was incorporated in 1640. It was here that Daniel Webster was finally laid to rest. A short drive brings us to Green Harbor. Marshfield shores are very attractive to sportsmen. Sea ducks and shore birds abound. Cut River and Brant Rock are some of the most noted places. Brant Rock is noted as a healthful and delightful summer watering place. Many very distinguished people come here to spend the summer months.

COPYRIGHT 1891. A. S. BURBANK, PLYMOUTH, MASS.

Ancient Winslow House, Marshfield, Mass.

Marshfield Hills and Sea View are also very attractive summer places. It was at Marshfield that Edward Winslow first settled and called his place "Careswell Place," after his English estate. Daniel Webster came to Marshfield in 1827, and after living here five years he finally purchased an estate belonging to a revolutionary royalist, where the British soldiers were stationed in the war. This fine old mansion he took great pains to adorn with lawn and shade trees. But a few years after his death the house was burned.

Daniel Webster Place, Marshfield.

Grave of Daniel Webster, Marshfield, Mass.

Duxbury Library.

View of Duxbury Bay

And Powder Point Hall, from Mr Knapp's.

and a house built of timbers of the old house by his grandson, is to-day one of the most noted places in the town of Duxbury. John Alden lived to a great age, and singular it is to relate, there has always been a John and Priscilla from the original stock. Myles Standish's son married John Alden's daughter, so two of the grandest and most noted families were united in marriage.

One of the great attractions in Duxbury is the new bridge connecting the main land to the neck of land known as Duxbury Beach. Here we have a commanding view of the ocean, and a full view of Plymouth, Gurnet Light, and Powder Point. George Soule, of the "Mayflower," was one of the first settlers on this point of land. It is supposed Powder Point was named by the famous John Smith. Many are the ships that have been built on this point of land, which is now noted as a fashionable summer watering place. Another point of interest in Duxbury is the main street, running parallel with the bay, making a delightful drive, there being such a fine water view. Beautiful trees, overarching, and its old colonial houses, makes it exceedingly picturesque. In this village we find a library and one of the largest Odd Fellows' Halls in the state. It has lately been erected in this place.

Residence of Dr. N. K. Noyes, Duxbury.

Office of Anglo-American Cable Co., Duxbury.

Street View, Duxbury, Mass.

Looking north from Captain Cushman's Cupola.

Odd Fellows' Hall, Duxbury, Mass.

203

Residence of John A. Irwin, Duxbury, Mass.

Summer Residence of Alfred S. Foster, Duxbury, Mass.

Residence of Orson M. Arnold, Duxbury.

Residence of W. S. Freeman, Duxbury.

Duxbury village! Nature's fair resort
For those who wish to shun the city's din.
No fairer spot on God's green earth, for thought
Or poet's muse, than here, within
This ancient town where Standish lived and died,
And Alden brought Priscilla as a bride.
Here pastures green and sunny slopes, incline
Towards landlocked bays, where yachts in miniature
Float on the tide. While from the odorous pine
To invalids is wafted Nature's cure.
Ho! weary business men in search of rest!
Ho! invalids with days and nights of pain!
Come where the goldfinch robin builds her nest,
And fills the morning air with glad refrain.
Come where the bluebirds sing 'neath cottage eaves,
And whisper of mutation in their tones.
Where yet no foreigners, no rogues or thieves
Have marred the beauty of New England homes.
Here pitch your tents beside this tranquil bay,
Where silv'ry waters gleam in summer's sun,
Come, business men and women, sad or gay,
And we will give you welcome, every one.

Original Poem by W. S. FREEMAN.

Residence of Capt. George Cushman, Duxbury, Mass.

Congregational Church, built in 1844, Duxbury.

Looking south from Captain Cushman's Cupola, Duxbury, Mass.

Residence of Sanford Windsor, Duxbury.

Summer Residence of Lawrence P. Soule, Duxbury.

Duxbury view, showing Cassius Hunt's residence, in front.

Duxbury Yacht Club House.

The Duxbury Yacht Club was incorporated in 1895. The club house was built at the Standish Shore, which was occupied by the club two years. Desiring a more central location, a new house was built in 1897 by Cassius M. Hunt, which was leased by the club for a term of years. The club is in a flourishing condition, having a membership of over one hundred. During the season there are several regattas, and several new yachts have been added this year. The present officers: — Capt. George P. Cushman, Commodore ; Sanford C. Windsor, Vice-Commodore ; D. D. Devereux, Secretary and Treasurer ; W. M. MacDowell, Rear-Commodore ; A. E. Walker, Fleet Captain ; L. H. Delano, Measurer. Directors : — George P. Cushman, Sanford C. Windsor, D. D. Devereux, S. B. Chaney, Chas. H. Alden, Chas. S. Clark. The club was organized December 13, 1894. Chartered February 25, 1895. The first Commodore was William Melbourne MacDowell ; first Vice-Commodore, John A. Irwin ; first Secretary, D. D. Devereux, and first Treasurer, Alfred E. Green.

"CHALLENGE CUP"
Presented By
Fanny Davenport.
TO THE
DUXBURY YACHT CLUB
1895

Held and won by W. Melbourne MacDowell for three successive years by Yachts "Fanny D.," 'Cleopatra," and "Rooster."

First Commodore of Duxbury Yacht Club, William Melbourne MacDowell.

The Mudjekeewis, South Duxbury. Mrs. D. A. Banister, Proprietor.

Though the ancient prosperity of Duxbury passed away with the ships and sailors, after a period of rest the old town has renewed her youth, as a summer home for her old families — and for others who find the quiet life here so pleasant that they stay and come again — and so her bay is again made lively with summer sails, with regattas of her yacht club and with moonlight parties. New houses are building. The Rural Society has beautified the ways with trees, the public lands in the woods are being converted into a Park, and an air of thrift pervades the town with a sense of comfort and well being.

Residence of Mrs. W. Melbourne MacDowell, nee Fanny Davenport,
South Duxbury, Mass.

Yachting on Duxbury Bay, showing W. Melbourne MacDowell's Yacht "Fanny D."

Residence of Dr. Ira Chandler, South Duxbury.

Duxbury retains much of the flavor of the olden time, and presents most attractive pictures to the artistic eye, with its beach, bay, mossy hills and flowery fields, its pine woods, ponds and pretty streams.

In the western part of Duxbury is the corner which rejoices in the name of "The Tree of Knowledge," where long ago stood a hollow tree in which was deposited the mail from Duxbury and surrounding places to be taken up by the Boston stage on its way from Falmouth and Plymouth.

This island is still inhabited by descendants of its Pilgrim settlers, and is a rich farm with a climate so mild that figs can be ripened there. Though Standish and his house have long since passed away, Captain's Hill still ennobles the bay, and at its foot stretches a pleasant beach where the Standish House and many cottages tempt the summer visitor.

Myles Standish Monument, Duxbury.

The Standish Monument built in honor of the memory of Capt. Myles Standish is next to the tallest structure in the country. It is situated on Captain's Hill on the old Standish farm, where the old Captains lived and died. In 1872 there was a movement made to erect this monument, the ground previously having been dedicated in 1871. The first earth was broken in June 17, 1872, and the foundation was laid the following August, and in October, the same year, the corner-stone was laid with grand military and Masonic ceremonies in the presence of thousands of people, President U. S. Grant presenting to the monument the keystone of the arch, representing the United States. The cost of the structure completed will be $75,000. It is one hundred feet from the ground to the parapet. The top of the hat of Myles Standish above sea level is about three hundred feet. This monument can be seen for miles around in the surrounding villages.

Cottages on Miles Standish Shore.

In the early history of the country, Duxbury was renowned for its shipbuilding, the timber being taken from the neighborhood ; which even now has *eighty-five miles of wooded drives.* Truly a location combining country and seaside.

There are many ponds and lakes within driving distance. On one of the largest, "Silver Lake," there is a private grove for use of The Miles Stand'sh guests. The fields and woods are dotted with low gray houses characteristic of the locality. They seem made to fit the landscape,

spreading broad to the sun, and often enriched within by quaint old furniture and curiosities brought by sailors from foreign lands. In the pine woods are rambling roads and paths, bordered in spring by the pilgrim's mayflower and in summer by the wild rose and azalea.

Alexander Standish House.

Within a short walking distance is the Standish House, built in 1666, and the Standish Monument, finished in 1889. With the exception of the Washington Monument, this is the highest pedestal erected to the memory of a single person. The Standish House was occupied by Alexander, the son of Myles Standish, who married the daughter of John and Priscilla Alden; names which have become household words through Longfellow's poem.

COPYRIGHT 1896 by C. E. BOLLES.

The Grave of Myles Standish.

222

Partridge Academy, built in 1843, Duxbury.

Former residence of Augustus Weston, owned and rebuilt by E. G. Perry in 1896.

Public Library, Kingston.

Residence of Alexander Holmes, Kingston.

Town Hall at Kingston.

Residence of Horatio Adams, Kingston.

A village on a high elevation of land overlooking the bay, with well-laid-out streets and elegant residences. From here we have only three miles to make when we arrive at the ancient old town and landing place of our forefathers.

Major John Bradford's House, 1675, Kingston, Mass.

The homestead of Maj. John Bradford at Kingston, Mass. This house now stands on the original site, built by the grandson of Gov. William Bradford in 1675, who lived there until his death in 1736. History informs us that during King Phillip's War, this ancient residence was set on fire by the Indians, but was finally saved before much damage was done.

The Winslow House, built in 1774 by Edward Winslow, great-grandson of Governor Winslow, who came over in the Mayflower. After many years of hardship, the Winslows departed from the colony in 1770, and the house was then sold. The lindens now by the front door were planted by Edward Winslow's daughter. The rooms are high and very commodious, showing that our forefathers were as thoughtful for health and fresh air as we are at this day.

Village View at Kingston.

Main Street, Kingston.

227

Court House, 1820, Plymouth, Mass.

The Court House in Plymouth ranks as one of the finest in our state. It was built in 1820, but was remodeled and made more conspicuous in 1857. Architecturally a fine and magnificent structure, surrounded with a beautiful well-kept lawn and elegant old trees.

Samoset House.

Memorial Methodist Church, Plymouth.

National Monument to the Forefathers, Plymouth.

The National Monument stands as a memento to the honored bravery of our forefathers. The corner-stone was laid in 1859 ; the main pedestal was put in position in 1876, and the grand structure was completed in 1888. It is built of solid granite, which came from Maine. It is 216 times life size, and weighs two hundred tons. It was a gift from the Hon. Oliver Ames, of Easton, formerly a native of Plymouth, and cost over $30,000 to build. It represents Morality, Education, Law and Freedom, each wrought on a separate block of granite. In visiting Plymouth no one should miss seeing this beautiful work of art.

Street View, Plymouth, showing Memorial Church.

Old Colony Club House, Court Street, Plymouth, Mass.

Plymouth High School.

Plymouth, as an antique and historical village, is not only noted for those points of interest for which summer tourists visit this locality, but for its beautiful streets, its fine body of water, with its fine boating, fishing and bathing. With its natural quaintness, it is unsurpassed as a summer watering resort.

The sword, pot and platter used by Myles Standish is now on exhibition at Pilgrim Hall, and the travelers will find it to their advantage to visit this place, there being here on exhibition many of the original relics of the Mayflower.

Watch Tower, Plymouth. To the north

Sword, Pot, and Platter of Myles Standish.

Site of the Watch Tower in 1643.

of the old fort we notice a tablet, marking the place where the old brick watch tower was erected in 1843. Stone posts as boundaries give the dimensions of the old structure. The old hearth stone used by the forefathers, where they built their watch fires, still remains. Here many antique and amusing headstones may be seen.

Mayflower in Plymouth Harbor.

History teaches us that in the old country our forefathers had been denied the privilege of serving God in a manner suited to their tastes, and for many years many indignities had been heaped upon them, and a faithful few banded together, deciding to brave the dangers and hardships came across the Atlantic, and secured the goal of this New England coast, so plainly visible to the eye of Columbus, but not so visible to others. Finally, after much delay, the Mayflower was chartered, and 120 people started for the new world in two small ships, Speedwell and Mayflower.

After leaving Plymouth, the two small boats encountered very rough weather. The Speedwell sprung a leak, and both ships put back for repairs. Again they started. Still the Speedwell proved unsatisfactory, and they returned to port again. Eighteen of her crew decided not to cross the Atlantic. Finally the Mayflower started on this long voyage with 102 passengers. The little ship was of only 180 tons burden, consequently many inconveniences had to be overcome. William Butt died on the voyage, and a son of Stephen Hopkins was born on board the ship. They finally arrived and cast anchor in Provincetown on the 11th of November, after a passage of sixty-six days. They first sighted the cape November 9, but it looked so uninviting, they took council among themselves, and finally decided to steer clear of old Cape Cod and to make the Hudson River, but the wind changed, and the little Mayflower found Cape Cod, as our mariners do to-day, a dangerous coast. Finally, the wind and waves being against them, they turned about and steered for the cape. After coming to anchor at Provincetown, eighteen of the officers and men went on a scouting expedition, and the first night after leaving the ship was spent in Eastham; the second night in Brewster; the third night

Landing of the Pilgrims.

they reached Plymouth, spent the night on Clark's Island, which they named after the mate of the Mayflower, and the fourth day they rested, being Sunday, praising God for their deliverance to these quiet and peaceful shores.

Monday they found the harbor suitable to them for navigation, and on scouting the surrounding country found it planted by the Indians with fine fields of corn. They were delighted in finding many fresh water ponds and running brooks of water. Soon they returned to the ship, and remained in Provincetown until the 15th. Then they weighed anchor, and arrived in Plymouth Harbor, in just one hundred days from their first departure from Plymouth, England.

A most excellent view of the town of Plymouth is obtained from the summit of Cannon Hill. Looking down through the rich foliage of the green trees and shrubbery, we see intermingling beautiful ponds and water front, making one of nature's own delightful native views. It was

View of Plymouth Village from Cannon Hill.

The Gurnet Headland at entrance of Plymouth Harbor.

235

here that the first Indians met with our forefathers and exchanged gifts and tokens and afterwards signed the treaty of peace. Looking across the blue expanse of water one can see Clark's Island and the Gurnet Light.

Elder Brewster's Chair. Cradle of Peregrine White.

North Street, Plymouth.

Pilgrim Hall, Plymouth.

The Courtship.

237

Church of the First Parish, Plymouth.

The oldest house in Plymouth was built in 1660, and stands to-day as one of the ancient relics of this town. Many of the original timbers, which were hewn out of the oaks of the forest, still remain firm and are probably good for another fifty years.

Oldest House in Plymouth, The Doten House, 1660

The First Treaty with the Indians.

CLARK'S ISLAND. — This island is to be seen nearly across from the entrance of Plymouth Harbor. History says " it was here on the Sabbath morning that our forefathers first landed on this island, and spent the first Sabbath on the New England coast in praising and serving God," and miraculous, indeed, was the entrance of this little ship, the " Mayflower," to this then lonely and desolate coast. It was in a terrific storm, when every man aboard expected to have been lost, but through the Providence of God, they escaped after many hardships, and colonized then this " Land of the Free and Home of the Brave."

Clark's Island, showing where our Pilgrim Fathers spent the first Sabbath.

McPhail Pianos.

FOR FIFTY NINE YEARS.
MADE ON HONOR.
SOLD ON MERIT.

There are over 14,000 of these pianos in the homes of the best musical people of Boston. Endorsed by such musicians as Carl Zerrahn, John K. Paine, Louis C. Elson, T. Adamowski and Martha Dana Shepard. McPhail Pianos have received fifty-three awards of gold and silver medals in competition with the world's best makes of pianos.

A. M. McPHAIL PIANO COMPANY,
786 WASHINGTON STREET, BOSTON.

JONES & WILLARD,

... POINT INDEPENDENCE. ...

Livery, Feed and Boarding Stable.

 FOR FIRST-CLASS TEAMS AND GENTLEMANLY DRIVERS, THIS IS THE PLACE TO FIND SUCH A TURNOUT.. . . . .

NEXT TO THE BRIDGE, ONSET, MASS.

As the ORIGINATOR of YEAST or BAKING POWDERS in 1849, I was for many years the largest manufacturer of this class of goods until, through the competition from CHEAP and ADULTERATED ARTICLES, the alternative presented itself of either offering a similar quality of goods or abandoning the field. I chose the latter, and for years I have been out of the market; but now, through the revulsion of PUBLIC SENTIMENT AGAINST ADULTERATED GOODS, I am enabled to offer a NEW POWDER, which I have been experimenting with and perfecting during the interim.

I RECOMMEND this POWDER as ABSOLUTELY PURE — it contains neither Alum, Lime, nor other Injurious Substances, and is unexcelled by any in the market.

B. T. BABBITT.

JOHN W. F. THROCKMORTON,

NEW ENGLAND AGENT.

One quarter pound cans, 10 cents.   One half pound cans, 15 cents.

One pound cans, 30 cents.

Use B. T. Babbitt's Best Baking Powder.

FOR SALE BY ALL GROCERS.

BE WISE.   USE THE BEST.   IT PAYS.

BOSTON OFFICE: 35 CENTRAL STREET.

W. H. HERVEY & CO.

5 UNION STREET, BOSTON.

We Allow Freight to any Railroad
Station in New England. . . . .

This carriage, as per cut, upholstered in durable coverings, satine ruffled parasol, this year's style, wood or wire wheels. Price, $6.75. Terms, $1.00 down and $1.00 per week. Send payment down of $1.00 with order. Our new carriage catalogue sent free upon application.

BICYCLES.

We sell the best medium-priced wheel on the market. Large tubing, barrel hubs, 1898 model, weight 24 lbs. Call and see before purchasing elsewhere. Price, $45.00. Sold on instalments.

REFRIGERATOR DEPARTMENT.

Outside — Ash, Antique Finish.
Inside — Zinc, with wood Backing.
Walls — Packed with Charcoal, with Heavy Paper each side.
Ice Chamber — Galvanized Iron, Flat Bottom, with Corrugated Ice Rack.
Shelves — Galvanized Iron, Slatted.
Trimmings — Polished Brass.
Casters — Iron, Bronzed.
Price, $5.75.

Sole Boston Agents for the celebrated Jewett Refrigerators, 40 % discount. Terms, $1.00 down and $1.00 per week until paid. Send Cash, or first payment of $1 00 with order.

CARPETS.

A New, Fresh Stock of all the latest patterns in Ingrains, Tapestries, Brussels, Velvets and Moquettes. 200 patterns to select from. All goods sold on instalments if desired. Free delivery.

Parlor Suits, from $25.00 up. Chamber Sets, 10 pieces, from $14.75 up. Carpets, 200 patterns to select from. Sideboards, Chiffonniere Beds, Ranges, Parlor Stoves, Dinner Sets, Lamps, Blankets, Comforters, at Bottom Prices. Lower than the lowest.

WRITE FOR NEW CATALOGUE.

KENDRICK HOUSE.

WAREHAM, MASS.

 HIS house is situated in the quaint old town of Wareham, on an elevation overlooking the village, presenting a magnificent view, with the Waukinko River in front. It is a quiet, restful place, making a most desirable location for those wishing rest and quiet during the summer months. Large areas of pine grow in the vicinity, the odors from which, intermingling with the salt air from the ocean, make a combination both invigorating and healthful. The woodland drives are very attractive, and many points of interest are within easy driving distance. The roads are excellent for wheelmen. The house is comfortably furnished, rooms are airy and large. Good facilities for fishing and boating. Good stable connected. For particulars, address the Proprietor,

MRS. A. B. MERRILL.

LORING BROTHERS,

Livery and Boarding Stable, ❧ ❧ ❧ ❧

WAREHAM, MASS.

The above firm are the recognized leaders in Livery, and are ever ready to furnish fine turnouts, with good variety of fancy carriages, and fine horses can be found here to be let by the day, week, month, or season.

A full line of harnesses, blankets, robes, and whips, always on hand for sale.

HE only store in Southeastern Massachusetts where customers can have all needful demands supplied. ✦ ✦ ✦ ✦ ✦ ✦

E. N. THOMPSON & CO.,

 *Dealers in*
Foreign and Domestic Dry Goods; Small Wares; Fancy Articles; Ready-Made Clothing; Gentlemen's Furnishing Goods; Boots and Shoes; Carpeting and Upholstery Goods; Paper Hangings and House Furnishings; Hardware and Farming Tools; White Lead and Oil; Choice Groceries; Flour, Grain and Hay; Hair, Lime and Cement.

CUSHING HOUSE, Hingham, Mass. ❀

GEORGE CUSHING, Proprietor.

This is one of the best equipped, arranged, and well-kept hotels on the South Shore, only seventeen miles from Boston, making this a very desirable place for a homelike hotel near the city.   For full particulars address the proprietor, Hingham, Mass.   .   .

PACIFIC HOUSE,

☙☙☙ NANTASKET BEACH, MASS. ☙☙☙

To former patrons a description of the location of this Hotel is unnecessary, but we would call the attention of the public to its numerous and varied attractions. The House is situated on a rocky prominence, surrounded by a broad piazza and commanding a full view of the Atlantic Ocean, Boston Light, the famous Minot's Light, and in close proximity to delightful and picturesque walks and drives, and is pronounced by all the paradise of New England.

Connected with this House are a beautiful Music and Dance Hall, Summer Houses and Bath Houses. A commodious livery stable is also connected with the House where patrons may be accommodated at reasonable terms.

Communication in regard to rates, or other information, will receive prompt attention.

MORIN & SCHUBIGER, Proprietors.

NANTASKET BEACH, MASS

House Opens May 15th.

Black Rock House,

...NANTASKET BEACH...

This hotel, occupied as such during the summer only, stands on a high, rocky prominence about fifty yards from the shore front, and opposite some of the finest estates in this vicinity. It commands an extensive view of Nantasket Beach, Minot's Light, and has a full range of the nearby points of interest, getting even the slightest breeze from the harbor and bay. Its situation is cool, open, and pleasant. Its drainage is perfect, rendering the location one of the most healthful and desirable on the New England coast.

The manager spares no pains to secure the comfort of his guests, and to make this Hotel their home while here.

.... N. R. SMITH, Proprietor.

FRANK W. BROWNE,

DEALER IN ....

Drugs, Medicines, Toilet and Fancy Articles.

PURITY, ACCURACY AND SKILL

Are the three essentials in COMPOUNDING PRESCRIPTIONS. All of these you get by having your work done at

BROWNE'S PHARMACY,

ESTABLISHED IN 1878,

SOUTH MAIN STREET ✧ ✧ ✧ ✧ ✧ COHASSET.

The Cliff,
North Scituate Beach.

 THIS commodious and Popular Hotel of seventy-five guest chambers was built in 1896. Its commanding position on the Bluff gives it magnificent views of the Ocean and the Beach and, inland, of the country and Cohasset Harbor.

The House is thoroughly modern in its construction and appointments, with spacious piazzas and dining-hall, and parlors with fire-places and steam heat, a pure water supply, sanitary plumbing, electric lights and Public Telephone. Best facilities for Bathing, Boating, and Fishing. Also Boarding and Livery Stable.

The Cliff is managed by its owner, Mrs. Mary R. Cushing, and is open from June 15 to October. The furnishings and table are first class Rates $2.50 to $3.00 per day, and special rates by the month or season. P. O. address, North Scituate, Mass.

Ḣotel Stanley ❧ Scituate Ḣarbor,

IS THE LEADING HOTEL OF THIS FINE OLD
SOUTH SHORE VILLAGE.

Scituate Harbor is an old-fashioned New England sea-coast village, with a fine harbor, on which the government has expended many thousands of dollars. For bathing, boating, and fishing it is without an equal on the New England coast, and its beautiful country drives and many sightly hills give it a peculiar attractiveness as a summer resort. On its coast are four high elevations of land, known as the cliffs, overlooking busy Massachusetts Bay. Its own waters are teeming with the many graceful spritsail boats of fishermen and the gatherers of Irish moss, and the sandy beaches are dotted with their cottages and moss houses. In short, Scituate Harbor is the ideal Old Colony town.

Hotel Stanley is located in the center of the village, and patrons will find it a neat, comfortable, and well-managed hostelry.

For particulars as to rates, etc., address

WM. STANLEY, Proprietor.

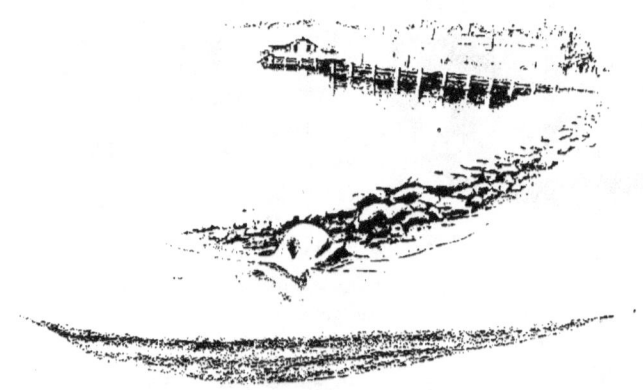

The picture on page 200 shows Powder Point Hall, which is the main building. The grounds are large, and have groves and shade trees, and open fields for sports. They extend to the bay, where is the old King Cæsar's Wharf. The Duxbury Beach is reached by crossing Gurnet Bridge, where there is surf bathing.

Summer Cottages to let or for sale. Building Lots for sale. These are at Point End and at Abram's Hill.

F. B. KNAPP.

W. S. Freeman and Co.

For three decades this house has held its trade,
And kept the town supplied with all it needs ;
And still with varied stock and prices low, still leads,
Defying competition ; not afraid
To quote with any firm along the shore
Or in the State, who keep a country store.

We thank our many patrons for their aid,
In keeping in this town so large a stock ;
And as we don't believe in wasting talk,
We simply ask the patrons we have made,
To call and see our stock of ninety-eight.
It's full in every line, and up to date.

THE ST. GEORGE HOUSE,

❋ ❋ ❋ DUXBURY ❋ ❋ ❋

This beautifully located House stands in the center of the village, only a short walk from the beach. Rooms large and airy, wide verandas, fine lawn, and nice stable connected with the House. At this Hotel the proprietor always makes it a point to have the people well pleased. Terms reasonable, and special rates by the season. Catering for parties or private families.

GEORGE W. SCOTT, Proprietor.

WINDSOR & PETERSON,

DEALERS IN

❧ Choice Family Groceries ❧

Our customers will always find in this store a full and complete line of Foreign and Domestic Groceries. This is one of the oldest and most central stores in Duxbury, and our aim is to be up to the times and in the swim. We make a specialty of having in stock the famous Diamond Butter.

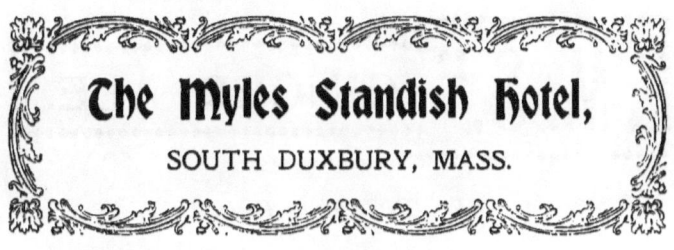

The Myles Standish Hotel,

SOUTH DUXBURY, MASS.

The most charming seaside resort in historic Plymouth County, only thirty-nine miles from Boston ; recognized everywhere as one of the most beautifully situated, superbly equipped and successfully managed hotels on the continent. The patronage is of the best, and the attractions are without limit. Every detail of indoor entertainment and outdoor sport is carried to complete perfection.

THE FINEST HOTEL GOLF-LINKS IN NEW ENGLAND.

Open from June to October.   Write for illustrated booklet.

RAYMOND L. COVERT, Manager,   L. BOYER'S SONS, Proprietors.
169 Devonshire Street,   90 Wall Street,
Boston, Mass.   New York, N. Y.

"M. S." GINGER ALE.

A NEW ENGLAND PRODUCT.

Surpassing in Excellence all Imported and Domestic Brands.

THIS Ale is made at South Duxbury, Plymouth County, Massachusetts, with the celebrated MYLES STANDISH SPRING WATER, which, owing to its unequalled softness and purity, is peculiarly adapted for the purpose. In conjunction with it are used only the very best quality obtainable of Jamaica Ginger root.

"M. S." Ginger Ale is guaranteed to be entirely free from all adulterants and impurities and the greatest care is used in compounding, to insure an article of the highest grade.

The popularity of the MYLES STANDISH SPRING-WATER is based on its medicinal value. It is second to none, if not superior to any waters in the world, and is endorsed by the MEDICAL FACULTY AND THE PUBLIC as an absolutely pure and perfect water, and remarkable for its solvent properties.

Information and literature concerning the famous MYLES STANDISH SPRING, or MYLES STANDISH HOTEL, will be gladly given at our depots, 169 Devonshire Street, Boston, Mass., or 90 Wall Street, New York, N.Y.

L. BOYER'S SONS, Proprietors.

❧ Samoset House, ❧

Court Street, Head of Railroad Park, Plymouth, Mass.

D. H. MAYNARD, Proprietor.

A first-class hotel in every respect. Accommodations for one hundred guests. Commodious public rooms, steam heat, electric lights, baths, long distance telephone. Three minutes' walk from Pilgrim Hall or National Monument, and convenient to all other points of historic interest and the county buildings. Special rates for June and September.

CORRESPONDENCE SOLICITED.

Plymouth Rock House.

Is situated on a high bluff overlooking the harbor, and within a stone's throw of the historical Plymouth Rock. While other hotels may have good views, this house has the finest that can be found anywhere, having, as it does, beautiful lawns, with some of the oldest shade trees, intermingling with a beautiful water view. It is unsurpassed for its coolness and the home comforts to be obtained at this hotel.

                                          *   *   *   *   * C. H. SNELL, Proprietor.

❧❧❧ A ONE IDEA STORE. ❧❧❧

This idea is to serve our customers with the best of everything in our line at reasonable prices, promptly and efficiently.

H. H. COLE,

35 MAIN STREET.

PLYMOUTH, MASS.

DO NOT FAIL TO VISIT THE OLD CURIOSITY SHOP
WHILE IN PLYMOUTH.

WINSLOW BREWSTER STANDISH,

LINEAL DESCENDANT OF CAPT. MYLES STANDISH.

Old Curiosity Shop, Winslow Brewster Standish, Plymouth.

Dealer in Ancient and Antique Furniture, Pewter Ware,
Crockery and China, Fire Sets, Old Books,
and a variety of ancient articles.

A large assortment of Views, Guide Books, and other Plymouth Souvenirs.

WATER STREET (near foot of Leyden), PLYMOUTH, MASS.

THE PILGRIM BOOKSTORE
PLYMOUTH, MASS.

Historic Plymouth.

Descriptive of the historic points and localities famous
in the story of the Pilgrims. Illustrated with many
half-tone engravings, and sketches in pen and ink.
A beautiful cover design in color, by Hallowell, of
John Alden and Priscilla. Price by mail, 25 cents.

Handbook of Old Burial Hill.

Its history, its famous dead, and its quaint epitaphs,
by FRANK H. PERKINS. Illustrated with pencil
drawings, sketches and tracings of the curious old gravestones to be
seen in this place of sepulture of Pilgrims and descendants. Price
by mail, 25 cents.

Plymouth Rock.

A souvenir booklet in photogravure. Twenty-four pictures of Ply-
mouth. Points of historic interest. Mayflower relics, Paintings in
Pilgrim Hall, Streets, Scenery, Old Houses. Descriptive page.
Price by mail, 25 cents.

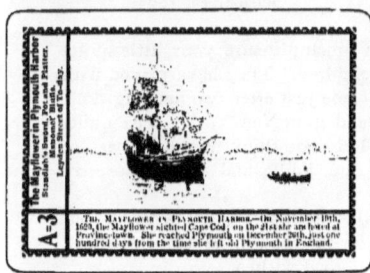

The Mayflower Game.

A new game, after the plan
of authors, consisting of fifty-
two cards, each one illustrat-
ing by a fine half-tone picture some historic place or
object in old Plymouth, or
some scene relating to Pilgrim history. Each picture
is accompanied by a short
descriptive text instructing
the player in the story of
Plymouth and the Pilgrims, the whole making an amusing and interest-
ing game. By mail, 25 cents.

Send for Illustrated Catalogue of Pilgrim His-
tories, Illustrated Plymouth Books, Photographs,
Souvenir Spoons, China, etc.

A. S. BURBANK, Pilgrim Bookstore, Plymouth, Mass.

I have some extra fine tracts of land for sale, where in a few years money invested can be more than doubled.

I have some very reasonable estates and some of the handsomest estates on Cape Cod for sale. I have them in nearly every location on the Cape.

Come in to my office and let me show you some of the fine places I have to offer.

E. G. PERRY,

50 STATE STREET ❦❦ BOSTON, MASS.

GRAY GABLES, Buzzards Bay, Mass.,
October 13, 1895.

DEAR MRS. PERRY: —

You do not know how much pleasure your little quilts have given my two older children. They have played with them constantly, and they came just after two new rag dolls were brought them by a friend from New York. The quilts and dolls just fitted, and I do not think they have been to bed since without Susie and Pollie and their respective quilts.

Little Marion is still rather young to enjoy her quilt, but her mother is very grateful for the thought of baby. I thank you very much, and with all good wishes.

I remain very sincerely,

FRANCES F. CLEVELAND.

This letter was received by Mrs. E. L. Perry, mother of the author of this book, she having made some little baby quilts for Mrs. Cleveland's children.

❧ The Hotel Pilgrim ❧

Beautiful Views.

Modern Improvements.

Excellent Cuisine.

Is pleasantly located on a high bluff, near the head of Plymouth Beach, commanding an unsurpassed view of both sea and land. The shore is easily accessible for bathing and boating. The scenery about the hotel is fine for artists with brush or camera, and lovers of nature delight in the beautiful walks and drives.

The hotel has extensive grounds, its own well-furnished stables, bowling alleys, billiard hall and tennis courts, and on its wide verandas one enjoys the cool breezes from Cape Cod Bay. It is furnished with steam heat, electric lights, pure water, baths, laundry, telephone connection, good service and a fine cuisine. Electric cars from railroad station to hotel. For particulars address

H. A. ROBERTS,
Hotel Pilgrim, Plymouth, Mass.

www.ingramcontent.com/pod-product-compliance
Lightning Source LLC
Chambersburg PA
CBHW030641030726
47497CB00006B/1901